CURSE OF THE SACRED WOLF

—⫘—

The Assassination Race II

Ronnie Stich

All characters and events in this book are fictitious. References to events, locations, organizations, incidents, and people are done so in a fictitious nature. Any resemblance to actual events or real persons, living or dead, is entirely coincidental.

ISBN: 0615881661
ISBN 13: 9780615881669

Visit www.RonnieStich.com or www.SecretAfterlifeSociety.com for more info.

Acknowledgements

I would like to thank all of my friends for their supportive words of encouragement. In particular, I would like to thank Shawn Terry and Adam Balderas for their valuable opinions of my work. Johnrobert Salazar is a great photographer and contributed with his artistic vision and media ideas for the future. I had some great research input from friends in various fields—Jason Armstrong, Carla Sanchez, Bill Rattay, and Brandy Leon. And, no, Eddie McAfee, I do not have the cassette tape I borrowed from you in high school.

To the guys from the band, Calabrese—you rock and I am a fan for life.

I would like to include a big thank you to the Whitehead Memorial Museum in Del Rio, TX for helping to preserve Del Rio's cultural history—including some of my own family history. The work your staff does is priceless.

Most important, I would like to thank Chris and my children for their faith in me. My sister, Becky, gave just the feedback

I needed. And also my mother, Kathi, helped tremendously in making this novel read the way that it should and kept me going along the way.

Death is not the worst that can happen to men.–Plato

▮▮▮▮▮▮ Police Department

Incident Report

229014451666

Date: Jan 13, 2013

INCIDENT DATA

Incident Location:
▮▮▮▮▮▮   Sa▮ A▮▮▮io   TX   7▮▮▮▮   ▮▮▮▮

Incident Type:
Threats/possible assault   Received by: Radio   time of call: 2359
Type of premises: Church   Domestic: No   Officer injured: No
Weapon(s) used: Not clear

VICTIM DATA

Name: ▮▮▮▮▮▮▮▮▮▮   Date of Birth: ▮▮▮▮▮
Race: Hisp.   Sex: M   Birthplace: CA
Address: ▮▮▮▮▮▮▮   S▮▮▮▮▮▮TX   ▮▮▮▮
Occupation: Church/Priest   Marital Status: Single

INCIDENT NARRATIVE

Witness called to report an assault on victim that started inside of church and carried on outside of church (witness data available on p.2). Upon arrival on scene, Victim refused to cooperate with police and asked that report not be made. Offender of assault described by witness as wearing black suit, black hat, and pale features. Witness stated that she could hear threats made to victim and that a possible gun was pointed at victim's abdomen. Victim refused to add to description of offender and denied involvement of any weapon. Victim had visible marks of attack on face and arms, refused EMS–was visibly shaken. Victim stated that he was visiting the church for personal reasons and would not elaborate. Offender left scene and was not apprehended.

After victim left scene, an officer (p.3) stated that victim asked privately again that report not be filed due to recent threats against his life. Officer was visibly shaken and light-headed, refused EMS. Details of officer's conversation with victim were not provided. Officer's condition was reported, details on p.3.

1

Congressman Fernando Montemayor's head ached and his mouth was parched. With his face pressed flat against the dirt, he inhaled a sour smell that forced a horrible vision into his mind. He was surrounded by humidity and darkness. The nausea quickened and took over, consuming every part of his being. It overwhelmed him as he propped himself up with shaky arms and shivered. There was something crawling in his hair. The large spider creeping through his thick, dark mane moved with a start, causing Fernando to slam an open hand onto the side of his head in reaction to it. After running his fingers through the rest of his hair to make sure the creature was gone, Fernando hunched over on all fours and vomited into the dirt beneath him.

As hard as he searched his thoughts, there was no real memory of what had happened. Only flashes of horror popped in and out of his mind. He looked out to the calm night water of the lake for answers, only to feel the nausea returning. His eyes were blurry. A gagging reflex in his throat distracted him momentarily as his eyes searched the abandoned part of the shore he had just awoken on. In the scattered branches and rocks, a rusted fishing hook caught his attention on the ground a few feet away.

"Jesus Christ," he croaked in a raspy voice as fragments of his memory now instantly returned to him. His arms were about to give out from weakness and shock. He rolled himself over so that he could collapse onto his back and away from the pool of filth he had ejected moments earlier. As he laid there, he looked up and saw leaves, full and heavy, rustling above like a thousand whispers. Fernando's eyes worked hard to focus into the massive trees. He could suddenly see the stars peeking through the branches, as his vision was returning to normal. And his memory was now rapidly getting stronger.

"No ..." he was able to groan. "No ... no ... no ..."

He had just enough strength to turn onto his side and look behind him to see if the pontoon was still out there, but there was nothing on the water but the moonlight. He needed to find the strength to get up. He wanted to find his car. He needed water. A primal thirst grew from within.

There was a bright flash, he was able to recall in the silence surrounding him. *They were ... standing ... in front of me. Looking at me.*

"No!" His face grimaced in pain and his mouth contorted. The throbbing in his head was indescribable, almost paralyzing. He pressed his hands to his face and realized that he was completely dry. His clothes and his shoes were dry.

My keys!

He reached down to feel for his pants' pocket and discovered his car keys, while unable to recall where his car was. The pain in his head intensified. Fernando felt that he was near the point of blacking out and covered his face again with his trembling hands. Tears started coming from his eyes and escaped through his fingers. He could hardly move his body and only had bits of faded memory about the ... *things* that callously discarded him on the shore of the lake— appalling memories that he wanted to claw out of his head. His body now convulsed with rhythmic sobs. His mouth quavered and gaped open beneath his hands just enough to beg for relief.

"God, please," he whispered between the tears. His vocal cords felt torn and raw. The dryness of his mouth made his tongue stick to his gums as he spoke into the night. "Don't let them find me again. I give myself to you ... let me die."

Six hours earlier.

The Texas sun had pissed him off all day. Its hellish rays blasted his skin, and he blamed it for ruining his attempt at fishing. After almost two impatient hours of destroying bait in moments of anger and fits of frustration, Fernando decided to maneuver his rented boat back toward the marina. Tossing back a few cold ones in the closest bar sounded a lot better to him than sweating his ass off on the lake.

"So you didn't catch a damn thing?" the older man behind the bar asked him with a crooked smile. His hair was white, and his belly looked to be quite round underneath the plaid button up shirt he was wearing. The shirt was understandably untucked, as Fernando was convinced that it would have been an impossibility for the man to wear it any other way with a belly sticking out that far—simple physics would not have allowed it. The man walked with a pronounced curve in his side that showed as he delivered a beer and a frosted mug to the congressman with a slow and tilted limp.

"It's hot as an oven on that lake. I can't remember the last time I went fishing." Fernando brought the mug to his lips before stopping abruptly as he seemed to recall something. "It was with my father. My dad fished this lake when it was known as 'Forney.'"

"Well now, that was a while back, sir," the bartender said.

"Sure was," Fernando agreed with a grin.

Now feeling some distant, yet sympathetic connection with the stranger seated at his bar, the bartender felt compelled to give him some friendly advice. He hated to see a suit like him, especially a political type, leave the area without some sort of bragging rights. It wasn't good for the man's inflated ego, and it certainly wouldn't be good for business. It only took one glance at the alligator insignia stitched onto the breast of the man's dark blue polo and the designer watch attached to his wrist to know that this suit had serious connections in the city. His dark hair looked like it had been a custom job, the color strategically picked to emphasize his brown eyes and dark plucked brows. He was definitely the type of man that used lotion on his face. They called it "metro-something." Either way, if he went back empty-handed, other metro-types might ignorantly assume that it was the lake's fault—not knowing what a serious priss the guy was.

"If you don't mind my advice, I could help you out a bit," the bartender offered graciously. He lowered himself to lean his arm on the bar top.

"What ... fishing advice?" the congressman asked with a soft chuckle.

"Sure. I can help you out. You'll leave the lake with some cats at least."

Fernando looked down at his car keys and contemplated staying the night in a hotel. He wondered if it was really worth fishing in the morning just to bring a few catfish home to the wife. He wasn't sure she'd know the difference between a fresh catch and his alternate plan to substitute them for a store bought version. She hated the things anyway. During their entire fifteen years of marriage, she had never once ordered them from a menu.

"I don't know if I can stay the night. My wife is already upset enough with me for coming out here on a whim. Got some wild hair in me and drove up here," he explained.

"Oh. I understand. But I'm talkin' about some night fishing. That's the best time to catch 'em. You wouldn't have to be out there too long. A black light might help in some parts, but you don't really need it." The bartender forced himself to stand tall in an effort to straighten himself. "Then you got some stories to take back with you to the city."

"Yeah," Fernando agreed with a sparkle in his eye. "None of those bastards at the office thinks I can fish. Of course, they'd be right. Can't hunt either."

They both laughed.

"After a few of these," Fernando said as he held up his beer mug with renewed confidence, "I'm going to get back over to that boat place, get my ass back on that lake, and catch some fish!"

Of course, that was before the lights from the sky blinded him a few hours later on the lake. And what happened between then and his waking up on the shore was a total mystery. Perhaps it was amnesia. He was lucky to be alive after blacking out like that—at least, that's what he would convince himself to believe … for a short time.

2

The crowd cheered as the starter emerged to begin the race. Both cars, a 1981 Camaro and a 1980 Trans Am, were ready and staged in front of the audience seated in the stands. Deidra loved it when a race fell on a perfect Texas night. It wasn't as humid as had been expected for May, and there was no rain in the forecast for at least another day or two. Of course, she would have liked it much more from inside one of those vampy, rebuilt race cars.

"I like how they painted that Camaro," Edward said to Deidra. "The deep blue is perfect. It's so sparkly."

Deidra rolled her eyes and frowned. They sat four rows up, just high enough to see everything. She made sure to wear a fluffy black skirt made mostly of tulle to replicate a feel from the 1980s over her black leggings. Her t-shirt and lace-up boots were also black. The shirt touted the name of a new wave band she used to listen to years ago—The Cure. The sleeves had been cut off, exposing the only colorful part of her look—the tattooed sleeves of classic paintings covering her arms. She didn't have to search around the local thrift shops for her outfit this time. The boxes toward the back of her storage unit labeled "my old stuff" contained everything she needed. Since Deidra's skin tone was already quite pale in comparison to others, the semi-gothic ensemble was naturally convincing, even though she refused to tease or change her jet black hair in any way to authenticate it further. A dark red lipstick and her usual heavy black eyeliner would have to suffice. And it did the job just fine.

The starter had dramatically risen from the first row and turned elegantly to wave at the crowd. He was a tall, thin man wearing a top hat and a cape lined in red satin. He took his place between the two cars and bowed to both drivers before turning to bow to those seated in the stands. He tipped his hat and pulled open his cape for them. On his hands he wore white gloves. The silky red lining of his cape captured the glow of the headlights in front of him. His face had been powdered in white makeup and his eyes darkened in black. He had painted his lips black too, and in his left hand was some type of walking cane that Edward initially believed to be a magician's wand.

"Who is he supposed to be?" Edward leaned over to ask Deidra. "Dracula?"

"No. I think he's just a creepy guy in a cape," she answered flatly.

The irritation in her voice was obvious to him, and he figured that it had something to do with the fact that he was wearing a suit from work instead of a costume … again. Deidra had tired of explaining it to him. It was the same conversation they had before every race. She would present some argument for the significance of costume-wearing and back it with some quantum physics-based particle theory—and he would simply wear a suit anyway. His reasoning always fell back on the professionalism excuse. But Deidra would suggest that he rethink that idea and explained that, by wearing a suit, he was dismissing the seriousness of the race and perhaps even making himself seem above others and its whole purpose. She asked him to consider suits from specific time periods and he said that he would consider it. When he arrived for the race in a dull two-piece from Saks, her face fell.

"This should be good!" a man in a cream-colored Miami Vice-looking blazer suddenly exclaimed in excitement. He was seated on the other side of Edward. The v-necked cotton shirt under his blazer pushed massive amounts of dark chest hair into view and made Deidra cringe.

"Yes, sir! It's a great night for it, too," Edward answered.

Deidra whispered into Edward's ear, "You see how Hairy Chest got into the spirit? And he runs a company bigger than ours, douchebag."

The starter then lifted one end of his cape into the air above his head and looked excitedly into the stands with his eyes, enveloped in every moment of his own dramatics. Silence descended upon the crowd, rapt with anticipation. The drivers, each of them dressed mostly in leather adorned with spikes and studs, looking a lot like they had been on tour with Judas Priest, gripped their steering wheels and readied their feet at the pedals.

The theatrical man before them pulled down on his cape with force, kneeling down with it to bring himself to the ground on one knee. He held on to the top of his tall hat as the racers flew past him. The two cars rocketed down the track, both of them showcasing behind them a hot blazing flame from their exhaust pipes. The deep roar of the engines and the heat of the flames could be felt by those seated closest with the greatest intensity. Any inter-planetary guests had been cautiously seated rows behind Edward and Deidra in an effort to respect their sensitivity to pretty much everything. Even from within their plasticky, quasi-human looking disguises, they always seemed to need extra special comforts and protection.

In the excitement, Deidra quickly rose to her feet to make her way down from the stands. She descended, stepping with caution onto each seat so as not to crush any fingers as she moved through and in between the oohs and ahhs of her fellow spectators. She paused on her way down to watch the ending. The glossy Trans Am had narrowly missed a tree for the win and she screamed in delight. As she continued to hurry towards the track, the man in the cape held his cane into the air, the tip of it pointing behind her and overhead in great exaggeration. Her boots touched the grass just as the crowd cheered so loudly that she could not make out the words coming from the starter's painted lips, but she did recognize the fear in his eyes and what looked a lot like, "Look out!" being said.

She turned just in time to see a black helicopter spinning in the air above the crowd. She screamed and pointed for Edward to look. As Edward stood to congratulate Mr. Cardwell on an excellently put together Trans Am, he caught sight of Deidra waving her arms wildly into the air and yelling at people to come down from the first few rows. People began screaming and rushing into the field before them in terror. Edward looked behind his shoulder and heard the sound of helicopters through the music that was now blaring from the loud speakers. He immediately pulled the two men on either side of him down through the bleachers by their arms, yelling for others to follow his lead. As Deidra noticed his efforts, she turned to run as far from the bleachers as possible. She ran toward the two racers, their faces frozen in shock.

"Go, go, GO!" Edward screamed as they ran across the field.

Deidra turned back to see how many people were still working to escape the stands just in time to see that familiar glimmer of transparency that would occur just after an extra-terrestrial vanished into thin air. The greys in the sixth row had escaped. The wave of humans, still desperately trying to flee the stands with their lives, had not. Many of them were still stampeding through one another, pushing and pulling each other along the way. Deidra had to turn away from it and braced herself for the horror as the spinning black heli-copter clipped another helicopter near it, and they both fell into the upper portion of the stands.

A set of loud explosions rocked them all and spewed fire throughout the field. Screams of panic and pain took over along with the pops of smaller explosions and the hums of the dying, twisted engines of the helicopters.

Edward was face down in the field until he looked up to see Deidra yards ahead laying on her side, gaping at what was left of the stands behind him.

Miles away.

"What the fuck?" the man with the shovel asked the man with the gun standing in front of him.

The man with the gun was looking over his left shoul-der at the ball of fire rising into the air in the distance. It was an odd thing to see in the middle of a barren Texas field. These parts, the outskirts of Dallas, weren't known for random, sensational explosions. It was known to be empty, quiet, and absent of activity of any kind. That's why he and the man with the shovel were there with the third man, who was dressed in women's lingerie, kneeling before them in a freshly dug grave.

The third man had his hands bound behind him and his mouth taped shut. The tape was wrapped all the way around his head several times in an effort of pure exaggeration. It was done to him in the same manner of taping-overkill that he had used on his last victim—before leaving her children without a mother.

The man with the gun looked down at the man kneeling in the freshly dug grave and shot him in the back of the head. He slumped forward, landing perfectly into his new eternal resting place.

"Leave him," the man with the gun instructed. His blond hair blew in the light wind, and the stubble on his face glistened in the moonlight.

The taller man with the shovel spit on the man in the grave. He then dropped his shovel down on top of the body with a clang as it hit what was left of the skull. He looked up at his partner with a smirk, knowing what they were about to get themselves into next. Andre, although more muscular and a bit taller than his leathery-skinned accomplice, always went along with his good friend's orders. No matter how irresponsible they may have seemed at the time, it always worked out for them in the end. Andre loved to joke intimately with his friend over drinks that he only did whatever he was told to do by the crazy white boy because he felt sorry for him.

Andre felt that he was certainly the more debonair of the two. His dark, handsome looks always seemed to charm the ladies of Dallas better than Nik's seemed to be able to. But jokes and friendship aside, Nikolas Vaughn was his superior.

The two of them jumped on their motorcycles and rushed toward the fire in the distance.

3

Fernando pushed through the trees and stumbled out onto the road. He fought past the weakness in his body to wave his arms above his head as he saw headlights approaching. When the car slowly pulled over, Fernando fell to his knees, relieved, and dropped his arms to the ground before him. He worked to catch his breath as a young man jogged across the road and stood over him.

"Are you all right? Do you need help?" the man asked cautiously.

Fernando lifted his head to look into the concerned eyes of the stranger.

"Do you want me to call an ambulance, sir?"

"Yes," Fernando begged. "Hurry. Get me out of here. Hurry! They'll come back!" He reached for the young man's pant leg to help steady himself and then looked into the night sky. "Please!"

On the outskirts of Dallas.

"We need every emergency backup you have in the area!" Edward yelled into his phone with a hand against his ear.

"They both crashed into the stands ... Yes, *both* of them. We need truck beds for cleanup. There are multiple bodies."

He looked around himself as panic and a gruesome realization took ahold of him. There were people lying on the track, slumped over in the stands, and scattered in the grass all around him. He did everything he could to keep his composure and stay focused. He looked for signs of life in bodies that didn't move—bodies that seemed too still. But he had to divert his eyes from the realization that some of them were, in fact, gone. It gripped at his soul with sheer cruelty, testing him. A woman's hair blew in the soft wind a few feet away, her hands placed over her face to cover desperate sobs. Where the woman sat, she was the only living human among the dead strewn around her. That is, until Deidra's team of paranormal investigators took notice and descended upon them like vultures.

Edward stormed over to her, stepping over legs and arms in the process. She was hanging over a man with a bloodied face. She had a digital recorder in her hands and was suddenly very annoyed by Edward's presence. "I'm busy," she said.

"This isn't the time for this!" he hissed.

Deidra rose from her knees and brushed herself off. She was covered in blood and her skirt was ripped. A large part of it hung loosely to the ground and was dragging in the dirt. She stepped closer to him, careful to prevent the man on the ground from hearing what she was about to say. "This is the moment before it happens," she snarled.

Two men near her stood only feet away holding their own recording devices over another severely injured man. One of the men paused to look to Deidra for permission to continue, and she waved at him frantically to carry on. The man's focus then returned more intently onto the man beneath him. He knelt down to get closer.

She started in on Edward with fury. "There is nothing we can do until help arrives, and since our help crashed down on us—"

"This is unbelievable! How can you do this *now*?" Edward spat. He turned away from Deidra and the two men assisting her on the morbid project to scan the activity around them. He saw that the same woman that had been sobbing in the grass earlier had changed her focus. She was now doing her best to drag a wounded man away from the stands, and Edward could see others that were trapped and needed help. He couldn't waste his time having a philosophical meaning-of-life type of argument with Deidra any longer and ran toward the shouting voices in the stands.

Deidra watched him blankly for only seconds and then returned to her work. The men assisting her had stopped to gauge her intentions—in case those had changed somehow in reaction to Mr. Bloodgood's sharp disapproval. But nothing within her had changed. Not her determination, at least. Edward didn't know about the last time she had captured a dying man's EVP—electronic voice phenomena. He didn't know about it because he didn't seem that interested when she tried telling him. It contained his dying wish—a wish she would carry out for the man.

"Keep going," she told her assistants.

He doesn't know anything. Maybe he'll never get it ... nothing in common.

There were over fifty people in need of medical care, and the dead were beginning to increase in number by the minute. Edward was at a total loss about how to handle the details. His only concern was getting it cleaned up effectively. As cold as it sounded in his head and felt in his heart, he knew that they needed to make it like they did not exist again very quickly. These races were a heavily guarded secret. Of course, all of this chaos was harder to focus on without Deidra's help. This was that part of her that he just couldn't connect with. It seemed more and more that she lacked any real concern for the living. It was just like her to put her version of science before the human suffering going on in the living world around them. But he could hear her argument for that decision playing in his ears already. It was a science that was studied to help save the human condition. It was essential, and only logical, that she make an effort to remember and recognize the importance of that research. Even in the face of the tragedy going on around them.

As the man she was having a recorded conversation with expired before her eyes, Deidra sighed heavily. She placed a gentle hand on the man's bloodied forehead and looked up to get an idea of what progress was being made by the rest of her team. She kept her recorder going even as she saw something she could not believe going on across the field in Edward's direction.

She immediately stood up and stared as two men on motorcycles made an entrance onto their private racing grounds and pulled right up to Edward. She shook her head and patted down her hip, searching for her phone before realizing that it was not there.

"Damn!" She looked at the lifeless man in front of her and knelt down to gently place the digital recorder on top of his chest. She pointed the microphone to his mouth. "Hey,"

she said to him. "Just say whatever you need to say. Um …
I'm sorry. I promise to check it later. There's just a lot going
on right now and … just do everything you can to let me
know what you want me to say to your family."

Several yards away, Edward stood firm as the blond-
haired man in the leather jacket got off his bike to approach
him with an outstretched arm. Edward did nothing to recip-
rocate the gesture. Instead, he stood taller, with his chin up,
as his dark tailored jacket flapped in the wind that was beginning to come in from the north. His glare was strong and
only grew stronger as the biker stepped closer.

"Who are you?" Edward asked angrily. He shifted his
eyes onto the other man who was still seated on his bike.

"Sir, my name is Nikolas," he began. "I know CPR and I
am trained in emergency response. My friend is also. Let us
help you."

"How did you get here?"

"We rode our bikes," the man replied with a hint of
sarcasm.

"No," Edward snapped. "How did you know we were
here?"

The races were not only secret, but they were illegally
operated, highly exclusive, funded (in part) by aliens, and
they weren't supposed to exist. Whoever this guy was, he
didn't have the right to be there.

"We were in the area and saw the fire." The biker held
open the palm of his hand and waved it in a semi-circle,
turning his body with it as he did, as if to remind the man
in the suit of the situation around them. "We don't have
time for a run-through of my resume, I think. I worked for
Mr. Andrews when he needed me, though. Let's just say that

he needed me a lot and that I know how to keep my mouth shut."

Franklin Andrews ... my psychotic predecessor. Excellent. "And you just happened to be in the area?" Edward studied the man carefully. His perfect posture was an unlikely match against his tattered jeans and studded leather jacket. His hair was a dark blond in the night, and messy. But his face was neat and clean looking, even with a bristly amount of hair beginning to peak through his weather-beaten skin. There was something un-thug-like about the man that was unsettling. His eyes were a sharp, light blue. And they were fixated on Edward while he was thinking of what to say next.

"Well, we were in the area ... taking care of something," the biker said as he opened up his jacket to reveal a handgun peeking out of a pocket sewn into the lining.

Edward looked behind him at the other man and then at Deidra making headway toward where they were standing. Trusting someone who was loyal to Franklin may not have felt wise to him, but Edward was in a serious bind, which became a major game changer. He extended his arm and they shook hands. "I don't have much of a choice. Anything you can do to help would be great. Thanks."

"Of course," Nikolas answered back. He signaled to his partner, and they both rushed toward a group of people lying on a grassy section to the right side of the track. The area had become a make-shift trauma center with people either being carried or dragged over for medical attention—and more of the injured were quickly joining them. People who were struggling to do whatever they could to comfort the injured, stopped as the two bikers ran up to them. After only seconds of listening to the two men, they rushed in all directions to carry out the new instructions they had been given.

"What did they want?" Deidra asked Edward as she watched the two men directing others within the chaotic scene a short distance away.

"They said they worked for Franklin. Do you recognize them?"

Deidra scrunched up her face before answering in a cautious tone, "Yes."

"I don't care who they are right now. I have more trucks on the way." Edward looked into the air and took a deep breath while running his hand through his brown hair. The color had faded from his face. His naturally rosy cheeks, which Deidra had always attributed to his anxiety-induced shyness, were pale. "I take over and then this happens. I just need this all cleared up. Get your ... ghost research guys to load some people into cars and go ahead and get out of here."

"You need to get out, too. The king first, remember?" she reminded him with a raised eyebrow.

"I will, but I'm staying until it's done." Edward was overwhelmed. The screams had jolted him deeply. There had been no time to think. There was only time for reaction. "They're sending backup." He swallowed hard. "And boxes to serve as coffins."

Deidra placed a hand on his arm and stood closer to him. "You are doing a good job. Be strong. I'll load as many people as I can into our cars and have a med team meet us at one of our warehouses. I guess whichever one is closest to town. You can send the rest of the injured there when we figure out the location."

"Okay. Call me as soon as you set it up."

"Eddie," Deidra paused as she turned away from him to leave. "Keep an eye on those guys ... the bikers. Send them away when they are done helping. Don't let them come to the warehouse."

"Okay," he said and turned to run toward the flatbed truck. It was being loaded with twisted pieces of the stands and melted helicopter parts. He wondered if this kind of thing would have happened to Franklin. And then he forced the thought out of his head.

Deidra scanned the area and stopped to focus on the motorcycles parked feet away from her. Then she looked again for their drivers among the crowd of victims strewn about the grass. She watched as they worked frantically to construct tourniquets and comforted those reaching out for them in pain.

It made perfect sense to her. They had been in the area on an assignment. Nikolas obsessively needed to have full control of the jobs handed down to his knights. It was more than just a personal control issue. He didn't trust very easily. He needed to be sure that things were being taken care of correctly because his name would be attached to it. In his line of work, he held himself up to the highest of standards.

He was the protected leader of one of the most notorious underground motorcycle clubs in the state of Texas. His reputation was riddled with malice and fear. His criminal resumé provoked uneasiness in anyone privy to its legendary history—except Deidra. And it didn't, and wouldn't, phase her one bit.

"Great." She shook her head in disgust at the thought of working with, or being connected to, these bikers and their crew. She wished Edward hadn't accepted their help and hoped to be rid of them very soon.

4

The next day.

"Twenty-six dead, three in critical condition," Edward announced to the group of men seated across from him. They were gathered at his home office—doubting and judging him on his own turf. "Those three are under heavy sedation, under the best medical care available, and are being guarded carefully."

"And the cleanup was successful?" one of the men inquired, looking to Deidra for an answer.

Edward had noticed during the course of the meeting that most of the questions being asked had gone right past him and were instead being directed at Deidra. He was understanding of that and even somewhat relieved by it. It was his first meeting with the more important government investors. He knew that they were used to Franklin's laidback, more confident approach to things. It was Franklin's desk they were seated at. Its grand design and ornate character was not what Edward would ever have picked out for himself.

"Yes," she answered from her seat beside Edward. "We sent a team to comb the area early this morning. It's clean."

The five men did nothing in reaction to her answer.

"I have logs and records of the parts we recovered," Deidra explained further. "Most of the bodies have been returned to their families for services. The appropriate cover stories have been supplied."

"It's a scenario we were prepared for, but never expected to put into action," Edward added nervously.

The men stared at him blankly until the one seated furthest to the left leaned in closer to him from across the oversized desk. "And there were no witnesses?"

Edward shifted in his seat. He ran his hand across his mouth and lightly touched Deidra's leg with his knee. He turned to her, hoping she would answer for him. He wasn't quite sure yet how much patience they had with him. The fact that Franklin had left him in charge of everything in the wake of his death was, so far, being respected by all the underworld crime elements he had dealt with. But Edward was still afraid that he was really just the company janitor in the government's eyes. There hadn't even been a welcome-to-the-club party or a hazing of any sort to initiate him. A simple cake would have been kind of nice.

And since Deidra didn't seem to understand his lame Morse-code-knee-taps to get her to start talking, he decided to answer them. "Uh, no ... I mean, I'm pretty sure that no one saw anything ..."

"A few members of the Secular Order were in the area," Deidra finished for him. She flipped her dark hair away from her shoulder. She had styled it into a side-part that reminded Edward of Veronica Lake. A darker, more deadly version of Ms. Lake.

Edward's eyes widened. "Right. Yes. Two guys showed up and they helped the injured until more of our own people arrived," he said timidly, trying to cover for himself. Now he felt more like the janitor's assistant.

"The Knights?" an older man on the right side of the desk asked with a start. The other men searched the eyes of their colleagues. They seemed to be confused. One leaned in to whisper to another and a series of nodding took place afterward.

Deidra then interrupted to explain further. "It was Nikolas Vaughn and his sidekick, Andre Clement."

The man to the far left slammed his hand down on the desk. "How were they just 'in the area,' Ms. Bonaparte? Does that make sense to you?"

"I really don't think they were watching us. I think they were as surprised as we were about what happened," Deidra explained. She made it a point to raise her perfectly arched eyebrows at Edward and then fluttered her smokey eyes at him. *See? I told you.*

"How do you know what their intentions are? How will they be kept quiet? We haven't hired them for anything lately. Who knows who they are under contract with right now?" the man pressed on.

Deidra stared into the patterns of the wood on the desk in front of her, thinking of a way to answer that might keep Edward out of trouble. "Nikolas was very loyal to Franklin and would never do anything to expose or ruin his dream of keeping the race alive." She sighed. "He would never betray Franklin."

"Here is the problem, Ms. Bonaparte," the man began without sending even so much as a glance toward Edward. "Our extra-terrestrial investors have tired of Mr. Bloodgood's cheapened, washed-out version of the races since he took over. They expect more excitement."

"I understand completely." She pressed her lips together nervously, knowing what was coming next.

"It's possible that this 'accident' was intentional."

Edward's heart jumped at the thought of it. "No."

"Yes, Mr. Bloodgood!" the man yelled in return. "Your racer qualification standards are fucking ridiculous! We *want* mentally unstable, dangerous racers! We *want* their criminal records to be a positive consideration—not a disqualification! You have ruined Franklin's race! The excitement is gone and your days are numbered!"

Edward hung his head downward and looked into his hands. He felt worse for Deidra than he did for himself. It was true that he had bent some of the rules. He had worked hard to convince Deidra to listen to him—to see his PG-13 rated logic. He now regretted every moment of it and was ready to return things to the way they had been when Franklin was in charge.

"Sir," Deidra began. "Mr. Bloodgood was thrown into this with no prior experience, but he is just as interested in keeping things profitable. We will do everything we can to please our investors."

"It's my fault and I plan to fix it." Edward lifted his head up and made sure to look into each of their faces. "I didn't understand before, but I do now. I didn't understand the importance of the risk and danger involved. I didn't work the books … I didn't know how much of this went into funds to preserve history, or to help medical research. I just didn't know about the emotional part of it … or the DNA … or the quantum level ... particle stuff. I'm still learning about worm holes and string theory. But I promise you, gentlemen, I intend to take it back to the way it was and fuck some things up again. Uh ... in a good way."

Deidra jumped in. "Yeah. We will return things to the way they were and look for better racers. We'll work to hire back some of the favorites. And we'll make it so losing a race will be worse than ever. The punishments will be ... *really* severe. We'll hand out envelopes with really good hit assignments in them—bloodier ones," she said excitedly.

"Part of the problem now will be trying to convince our investors to stay on board. For some reason they ... like you and Mr. Bloodgood. But they aren't happy with these new races. And they think the after-parties are boring," the man explained with an upturned nose.

"Too cliché," another one of them interjected. "They love Earth parties. At least, they *used* to."

"We'll set up a meeting and do a presentation. Whatever they want, we'll do it," she answered. "Eddie's good at presentations," she said with a sly smile.

"We'll set up the meeting and deal with them," the man offered with an agitated frown. "You just take care of the races. Make this next one impressive." He then turned to Edward. "Pray that they seem interested. Give them back the race they fell in love with. It keeps them entertained and off our backs when they visit."

"Yes, sir," Edward agreed wholeheartedly.

"Mr. Bloodgood," the man studied Edward carefully as he spoke. "I heard a terrible rumor that some of our alien investors have started seeking out and testing new human racers themselves. They are doing this in uncontrolled environments. It's an ugly universe out there. The rules are almost non-existent. Those quantum particles you referred to a minute ago can come in many different flavors. Some flavors are stronger than others and much harder to come by. It's like a psychic drug to them. We have to create a perfect condition for those particles to happen the way they do. If we don't supply them with what they want … here on Earth, they will find a way to get it someplace else."

"I understand."

"No, you don't. These are addicts, Mr. Bloodgood. Crazed, demented addicts."

5

Vincent Carracci had visited various emergency rooms three times already that year, and it was only May. It was a cracked collar bone in February and a laceration to the back of the head in March which only required a few staples. He didn't remember the visit in April very well since he had suffered a concussion. But in none of those visits had he been handcuffed to the hospital bed like he was this time.

"I have to piss," Vincent complained to the police officer who was slouched in the seat next to him. The officer was staring at the television, rooting for his favorite basketball team playing in San Antonio.

"You went ten minutes ago."

"Hey, it's not my fault they got an IV filling me up like this. I gotta go."

The officer looked him over and frowned. "They didn't give you a catheter?"

Vincent smiled. "They tried, but I got this horse dick that they don't got the right equipment for."

The officer laughed and then went back to staring at the game on the TV hanging in front of them. "Good one."

"Naw ... I told those bitches to get off my dick. I said, 'Don't you put anything up there or you'll regret it!'"

"You shoulda let them do their damn job. They were trying to help you," the officer advised.

Vincent then whined like a grade school child hamming it up for the teacher. He pulled his arm tight to clang the metal handcuff against the rail of the bed. He looked at the Dallas policeman's face to gauge his reaction and was disappointed when he didn't see one. "Come on!"

The officer simply yawned and glanced outside the door to the room. The fluorescent lights from the hallway glowed too brightly from where he sat in the dark. People rushed back and forth like blurs, making him feel like he was moving in slow motion. "The other guy will be here in a few minutes. I think you can hold it a while."

"I'm gonna piss the bed, Copper."

"Not my fault, Flight Risk."

"Awww ... but I didn't do nuthin'. They're all lyin' to ya," Vincent joked with a laugh. He put on his best mobster-movie voice, hoping to lighten the mood and gain some undeserved trust in the process. "What did they tell you about me anyway?"

The officer sat back in his seat and crossed his legs while tilting his head back. The game that had held his attention was going into half-time. He didn't mind an interesting conversation with a well-known repeat offender. Vinny the Snake was well liked within the department but not for the right reasons. His comical edge and easy-going nature made him a favorite when it came to arrests. At 26 years of age, he was reaching an unfortunate—but legendary—status. But it didn't mean that he was about to get away with any kind of ass-kissing, though. It was well known that he had earned his nickname from escapes.

"Street racing," the cop reminded him.

Vincent smirked and turned his body toward the cop in several exaggerated and awkward movements. It reminded Officer Garcia of a caught fish flopping around in a boat. "You guys chain people to beds for street racing?"

The officer looked at Vincent's greased hair and damaged face. Vincent looked as if he had just stepped off the set of a 1950s movie about hot rods. When he was arrested at the crash, he was wearing a mechanic's shirt with a name patch on it that read "Joe." His body had been crumpled and smashed against the windshield on the inside of his flat black, 1940 Ford Coupe, with blood running from his mouth and forehead. It wasn't until they wiped the blood off his face that they realized who he really was. The car he had smashed into was a 1942 Ford pickup, and the driver was missing.

"I was being nice when I called it 'street racing.' It's actually about ten different charges as far as I know. One of them is evading police during a chase. Another one is a possible manslaughter charge if we find a body somewhere out there rotting away." Officer Garcia shifted his eyes in Vincent's direction to catch his reaction. "You know we never found that guy from the truck."

"You're not going to find a body cuz there isn't one," Vincent defended himself adamantly. "He took off cuz it was his fault we crashed. And I didn't know you guys were chasing us. I thought you wanted to join in."

"Okay, well, like I said … just hold the piss a few more minutes until I have another officer here. That sedative they gave you seems to be wearing off."

Vincent shook his head and twisted his lips in protest. He took in a long breath through his nose and let it out forcefully. "You ever heard of people dying from holding it too long?"

"Well, you're in the right place if that's going to happen," Garcia reminded him as he waved a finger around the hospital room.

"Man! I'm being serious!"

"Of course, I've heard of that," he smiled. "It's *rare* and it's not happening to you. Just relax a few minutes and stop asking me."

Vincent stared at the policeman's face. His dark uniform was too clean and his shoes were polished. He guessed that he was in his late thirties and probably a bore. He couldn't imagine the man ever doing much of anything very interesting and was probably married to an equally uninteresting woman. Vincent imagined the officer to have a wife named Phyllis. He wasn't sure why, but that seemed like the right name for this guy's wife. He and Phyllis probably had boring sex every few weeks and always in the same boring position. They probably watched the home decorating channel, too. "I don't feel good."

Garcia rolled his eyes up to the ceiling. "What now, Vinny?"

"I'm serious, man," Vincent grabbed his stomach with his free hand and curled his legs close to his chest. He closed his eyes as tight as he possibly could in reaction to the burning pain that seemed to be emanating from his abdomen.

"This isn't going to work on me," the officer chuckled.

"Help ... me," Vincent pleaded. "Call a nurse!"

Officer Garcia turned in his seat to face Vincent. He bent over and leaned forward to get a closer look at his face. It was pale and contorted in pain. "Okay, I'll get one," he replied and he rose from his seat to push the call button on the bed. The look on Vincent's face frightened him.

As he stood over the detainee to assess the situation, Vincent used his free hand to grab hold of the policeman by the arm. The officer gasped and looked into Vincent's eyes in disbelief. He had grabbed him so quickly that it looked as if he had moved faster than light. The movement was unnatural and the grasp Vincent had on him was strong. The officer reached for his gun with his free hand, keeping eye contact with Vincent. The patient's eyes were glazed over, and the color was now cloudy. Even in the darkness of the room, Garcia could see that the life in those eyes had slipped away.

He drew the gun with his right hand and pointed it at Vincent's head and steadied himself. "Let go, Vinny."

Vincent opened his mouth. His tongue writhed and convulsed. He let out a deep groan as he slowly pushed the ghastly tongue, now coated white, out of his drooling mouth. His eyes began to flutter inside their sockets, but remained on the policeman, quivering before him. "They will have to close your casket for the funeral, Raymond."

The voice the officer heard coming from Vincent's mouth was not human. It didn't even match the movement of his lips. It was too deep and sounded more like two voices fighting to break out of Vincent's throat at the same time.

"Somebody help!" the officer called out.

"No one can help. No one can help. No one can help. No one can help ... no ... help ... for ... Raymond," Vincent hissed.

Officer Garcia's gun rattled in his hand. He looked up as the movement of people caught his attention at the open door of the room. He saw another officer, his gun also drawn, and a nurse, stepping in carefully. "Something's wrong with him! What do I do?" he panicked.

The nurse ran forward and pulled at Vincent's shoulder in an attempt to lay him down on his back, but he was stiff and too strong for her. She reached over his body to feel his forehead and jumped back. "He's ice cold!"

The other officer moved forward to hold down Vincent's feet, but also recoiled at the touch. "Jesus Christ!"

Vincent suddenly flipped onto his back and stuck his limbs out to his sides. He stared at the ceiling above them with bulging eyes and smiled. His skin appeared to have turned a light blue and his veins protruded. He licked his teeth before speaking. "Raymond Antonio Garcia … 38 … two children … enjoys grilling the flesh of animals and listens to rock music. His parents are dead. They were so proud of him when he joined the force even though his father said the scumbags helped cover up Kennedy's death." Vincent paused only to blink his eyes. "Ray? Does your father know about how you wrecked your little bike on purpose just so you could get a new one for Christmas? You wanted to be like the other boys sooooooo bad. You were sooooo bad, RAYMOND! RAYMOND, tell your father the truth! Tell him NOW!"

"He's fucking possessed!" the second officer yelled.

"Help me!" Vincent's normal voice returned as he managed to yell to them. Tears streamed down his face and his body shook. "Make it stop!"

The nurse ran from the room, leaving the officers alone and shaking in fear. Officer Garcia pointed the gun farther down to the arm that had a hold on him. He swallowed hard and tried to remember his responsibility as a servant to the community. He also tried to remember that Vincent Carracci was asking them for help.

"Please!" Vincent pleaded again. "Help me!"

The nurse ran back into the room and worked quickly to get a large dose of morphine into the IV attached to Vincent's arm.

"Let go of my arm, Vincent!" Garcia yelled. "I'm going to shoot!"

"WAIT! No!" yelled the nurse. "It's morphine! It's going to start working in a few seconds!"

The two officers and the nurse watched as Vincent loosened his grip, and the color began to return to his face. The tension in his body eased, and his eyes slowly closed. The nurse pulled him by the shoulder so that she could lay him on his back to rest. His fingers relaxed and his contorted face was returning to normal again. He looked peaceful, but wore a heavy crease in his brow.

Officer Raymond Garcia stepped back slowly and his entire body trembled. He gripped his gun with both hands and held it aimed toward the floor in front of him. The other officer remained at the foot of Vincent's bed. He looked at the nurse to read her reaction to what they had just witnessed, but all she did was hold her hands over her mouth and stare at Vincent. Her eyes were wide and glassy. A crowd of people in scrubs had gathered just outside the door. They were silent and afraid to enter the room, but watched frozen in horror.

Garcia knelt to the ground, one knee at a time. He shook uncontrollably. Tears fell from him, and the tip of the gun in his hand tapped against the floor.

"Hail Mary, full of grace, the Lord is with thee. Blessed art thou ... I ... I forgot the words ...I don't know what happened. I almost shot him. God, forgive me ... I almost *shot* him ..."

6

Meetings over lunch were the most ideal way to take care of business, in Edward's opinion. Any awkward moments of silence could be played down by the insertion of food into his face. Any questions asked of him that may require more time to answer could also be covered strategically in the same manner.

"Anthony made the arrangements, so stop asking me where they are," Deidra snapped at Edward. "They're probably in jail for all I know. And I told you that Feinstein was a freaking clone. One of him was. I don't know which one. I don't even know if clones eat food." Her voice trailed off in contemplation.

"Probably neither of him was a clone. Neither of them … either … whatever," he responded. "Who would want a copy of *that* guy?" He wondered why, after all this time, she was still convinced that "the real" Johnny Feinstein was actually dead. It's not like he was seen as a particularly good racer anyway. It was just that he was entertaining, self-destructive, and fun to watch. Even if he had been killed by Franklin, Edward just didn't see the incentive behind cloning him afterward. Johnny was a total mess. Making a copy of him just didn't seem logical.

She reached for the glass of water in front of her while looking toward the restaurant's entrance. It was a risk to recruit racers, and re-recruiting them into the game was even worse. Convincing them to come back to the race would certainly prove to be difficult since Edward had dismissed them. Deidra knew these guys. Their egos had to have been bruised as a result of Edward's harsh—and quite incorrect—decision making. Letting go of their best racers, just because they were hardened criminals, had been a terrible mistake.

Edward fidgeted with his tie and looked out the window. "Okay. There's Johnny."

"Fake Johnny."

"Whatever."

She scanned the sidewalk from her seat by the window and looked at the cars taking up the parallel parking spots. The street was busy with traffic and business people rushed to and fro, trying to make the best of their rigid and compact lunch hours. The café across the street was packed. It had been her first choice for their meeting, but Edward had been very specific. He wanted to buy the three men who would be joining them a nice convincing meal. Not a bagel and some frothy coffee.

Johnny walked through the door in a way that was more like an explosion, covered in a mix of leather, chains, and ripped denim. His combat boots were tied loosely to his feet so that they made even more noise than they should have as he stomped toward their table at the back of the dining room. He even took the time to slow down along the way to snarl at the wine steward.

Edward rose from his seat to greet him. "Hello, Johnny."

Johnny cleared his throat and brushed the palms of his hands on his shirt before reaching out to return the handshake. "Hello, sir," he replied weakly.

"Please have a seat. There's a menu there ... order whatever you like," Edward smiled nervously.

Johnny opened the menu and held it up to his face, covering himself just enough to still be able to see around the table. "What's up, D?" he asked.

"Are you seriously talking to me?" she asked coldly.

"Yeah."

"Don't call me that."

"Sorry." He cowered quickly.

A man then caught her attention outside the window as he passed by and waved. It was Tripp Raudive. He had always been courteous, well-mannered, and highly dedicated to the race. Deidra was glad to have an opportunity to get him back into the game—even if he had the kind of eccentric criminal record that might scare off most sane people.

"Tripp is here. We're only waiting on one more," she said to Edward.

Johnny groaned. "I gotta wait to order?"

"No," Edward answered with a wide smile. "Go ahead." He waved his hand to get their server's attention as Tripp was escorted to their table.

"Hey, Tripp!" Deidra stood to walk around the table to greet him with a hug.

"Deidra! It's good to see you, doll!"

Edward smiled and nodded as Tripp took an empty seat next to Johnny. Tripp then scanned the only other spot available in between Johnny and Mr. Bloodgood and wondered who else would be joining them. Both men sat across from

Edward, positioned so that the appropriate amount of eye contact could be made. He needed to be taken seriously. The races had to return to the way they used to be. Immediately.

Edward then whispered to their server and waited as Johnny placed his order before allowing Deidra to place hers. Tripp requested a few minutes more to look things over while insisting that he was okay for now.

"So," Edward began. "I like the blue hair thing you've got going on, Johnny. It suits you."

Johnny shifted in his seat. "Thanks. I got tired of the green."

"We have another guest on his way, so if you gentlemen would like to eat while we wait ... Vinny should be here soon."

"He's not coming," Johnny interrupted.

Deidra looked at Tripp in surprise and then to Johnny. "Why not?"

"He got arrested last night," Johnny informed them without looking up.

"For what? Prostitution?" Tripp laughed.

Johnny loosened up and laughed along with him. Deidra joined in as Edward placed his hand to his forehead to relieve some tension.

"... at your house?" Tripp added while looking at Johnny.

Johnny stopped laughing abruptly and frowned. "That's cold, man."

"All right!" Edward waved his hands across the table and leaned forward. "That's enough."

"Okay, okay," Deidra said, doing her best to catch the tears of laughter beginning to leak from her eyes. She used her finger and carefully wiped them away without smearing her eyeliner. "Mr. Bloodgood would like to talk to you, and later with Mr. Carracci, about getting back into working with us."

Johnny and Tripp looked at each other as Edward folded his hands on the table and tried to keep his nervous breathing under control. "We want you both to come back in."

"I don't get it," Tripp said to Edward. "Didn't you get new racers?"

"They're boring," Deidra explained flatly. "They shake hands, follow the rules, and they practice. The whole thing is stale, dry—and we're over it." She shook her head in disgust.

"Is it going to be the same as before then?" Johnny asked. "We race for some company and they pay us?"

"Hey!" Tripp jumped in. "What if we don't want to get back in again? You guys kicked us out like we weren't good enough for you!"

Deidra sat up straight and glared at him. "Seriously? Do you have anything else going on right now? I'm sure your arrest records aren't helping you get much work."

"Actually," Edward said as he sat back in his seat, a bit more confident he could convince them of his concern for their best interests, "It's going to be better than the way it was set up before."

"Explain," Tripp leaned in to say.

"There will be a small group of racers, the best in the country, selected to participate. Each racer will have his or her name on a chart with their stats, ranking them. The two best racers will always race. The company they represent will be determined beforehand. If you win it for them, they pay you a very nice bonus. If you lose, you still get your base pay, but your stats will be affected."

"What if we're racing against some company that we raced for in the past? What about those guys that try to pay you off to lose?" Tripp asked.

"Yeah!" Johnny chimed in. "They follow you around and threaten you to throw a race!"

"We are going to do our best to monitor things. If you can prove that someone tried to pay you off to throw a race, or threatened you, we will reward you," Deidra said in a serious tone. "And the punishment they would receive wouldn't be worth it. Trust me."

Tripp's eyes widened. "Does that mean we don't have to pretend to work for some asshole that we don't really work for? I hated that shit so much!"

"That's right," Edward smiled. "You can just race for them only when you are assigned to. You would be working for us instead. We can regulate things better that way. It was getting too complicated to let people choose their own racers. It's also a huge security risk."

"Plus, they would just stick you in the mail room most of the time anyway," Johnny added.

"The last guy I raced for let me kick people's asses for being late on accounts sometimes," Tripp bragged.

"What? How come you got all the cool bosses?" Johnny whined in response.

Edward looked at the two men and waited for their attention again before speaking. "But there's a condition. Since your loyalty won't be with any specific company, you will not be allowed to do any side jobs for any of them between races."

"How are we supposed to make any money then?" Johnny complained.

"The payouts are going to be higher," Edward explained. "Between races, I'm sure we can connect you with the right people. There's a lot of work in this city ... and others. Either way, you will be set up on our payroll."

Tripp looked at Johnny again and raised his eyebrows in excitement. Johnny reacted to him by shrugging his shoulders.

"Are you saying that we'll be on Society payroll?" Tripp whispered.

Edward nodded a firm "yes."

"How does it sound?" Deidra asked, knowing the answer already.

"I think it sounds good," Tripp replied cautiously. He was doing his best to hold back the excitement he was feeling. "How many racers will you have on board?"

"I think only five or six," Edward responded.

"Including me." Deidra grinned confidently.

"If you lose, you will not be allowed to race for two racing periods. This keeps the rotation going and keeps things kind of like it was before in that respect." Edward stopped to take a sip of his drink. "Not racing isn't going to be some kind of a vacation though. You will be assigned more jobs around town if we think you are slacking and less if you win."

"Society payroll means you can dump us in a lake whenever you are done with us," Johnny said with a scowl.

Deidra scoffed. "That blue hair dye must have leaked into your brain. Have you forgotten that we already got rid of you be—"

"Deidra!" Edward reminded her.

"How's any of this fair when it comes to her?" Johnny asked with a thumb pointed over in Deidra's direction. "She's your girl now, right?"

Deidra let a short burst of laughter break free and then reached over the table to grab Edward's hand. "Well, sweetie? Am I your favorite?"

Edward pulled his hand away gently and blushed.

"We're not a couple, smurf-head," she snapped. "And yes, I'm still going to do whatever the fuck I want, so get over it! I do *actual* work and have an *actual* job in a real building with an address and parking spaces."

"Doin' what?" Johnny asked.

She turned to Edward. "Let me shoot him."

"Deidra," Edward sighed.

"We can get other guys …"

Edward stood and extended his hand out to Tripp and shook his hand. "We have nice apartments set up for you both." He then shook hands with Johnny. "Thank you for coming back."

Deidra smiled weakly and turned to peer out the window she was seated next to. The gleam of chrome flashing from a motorcycle caught her eye. She leaned in closer to the window and squinted. The driver sat up straight, and robotically, wearing an open-faced black helmet and a white uniform.

"Right, Deidra?" Edward asked.

"Huh?"

"The apartments. They're pretty swank, right?"

"Oh, yeah," she answered, looking at Edward for only a moment before turning back to the window.

Gone.

Deidra decided to avoid the highway on her way home. Side streets just felt better to her. It would give her a chance to think about things she normally wanted to avoid. She never saw the point of cluttering her mind with unresolved issues—and it was unresolved issues that seemed to be forcing themselves onto her mind's center stage.

She came to a stop at a red light like she was supposed to. She sighed and wished that she had ordered an espresso at lunch. She was tired. Her father had called late the night before. It wasn't good news. Her grandmother was very ill. It took everything in her power to push the thought of life without her grandmother out of her mind, and the timing of it couldn't have seemed worse. The sting of happy memories plagued her more recently than ever. Memories of her grandmother cooking rice and tortillas in the kitchen with the windows open so that Deidra could hear her call when it was time to eat. She would play in the backyard while the grumble in her stomach interrupted her repeatedly so that she would ask, "Is it ready yet?" to the point of harassment.

Edward had called her on the way to lunch asking if she was okay. She knew she couldn't sneak it past him. Any time she was down, he was there to bug the hell out of her until she played confessional with him. His intentions were always good, but his methodology annoyed her at times.

She wanted to get home to her apartment for a few hours to rest. Edward expected her at his place that evening to go over some other issues their investors wanted taken care of. He had sweetened the deal with an offer to supply her favorite wine—a chardonnay made from the hand-picked grapes of a village in France named Meursault. It was a dangerous sign that he knew her too well.

As the light turned green she became engrossed with thoughts of Edward. She could see how much he had changed in the last six months. The naivety that once surrounded him had weakened. His distrust in the system had significantly increased. His face seemed to harden quickly when business matters arose. And his eyes had aged. Deidra wondered why she had not noticed the details of his eyes before and then forced herself not to. She dreamt about him recently and had been caught staring at him by Edward's assistant, the very forgiving Anthony. As much as she trusted Anthony, it was still embarrassing for her.

A flash of blue and red lights caught her attention in the rear view mirror. She slowed down for a few seconds to study the squad car trailing behind her before quickly turning down a street that might shake it off. "Damn!"

She slammed her fist onto the steering wheel and worked to maneuver her car as she sped up. After managing a number of difficult turns in an attempt to escape, she finally rolled to a stop in defeat in an empty parking lot behind an abandoned building.

The officer parked behind her and waited until a man in a white outfit pulled up on a Harley and jumped off of it as quickly as he could. Deidra flung her door open and stepped out angrily.

"What?!" she yelled. "Are you serious? You've got cops trailing me?"

She pointed at the squad car parked behind them.

"Give me five minutes," the man pleaded as he waved off the officer behind him. "That's all I'm asking."

"For what?" she asked in an exasperated voice.

"To tell you what happened," he responded. He approached her with his hands held out as if he was stepping toward a frightened animal. The heavily stained chef's coat he wore was rolled up at the sleeves to reveal several tattoos that were familiar to her. His hands were shaking as badly as hers and, behind his mirrored sunglasses, his eyes desperately searched her face for a chance to explain himself.

"I'm not someone you should pity," she warned him. "I don't care what you have to say."

The man's posture weakened as he removed his sunglasses and took another step closer to her. "Please listen," he begged and reached in to grasp her by the arms.

"Let go," she quietly asked and looked down in an effort to avoid his eyes. "Haven't you done enough?"

"Deidra, I was afraid of Franklin ... and things were changing with work. That's all it was. I couldn't do anything about it. My job ... he could have had my job taken from me over it."

He loosened his grip on her arms to remove his helmet and set it on top of her car.

She refused to look at him. "It doesn't matter," she began to cry quietly. "Franklin's gone now. I don't care what happened. I lose every person I waste my time caring for."

He waited a moment in the silence between them, hoping she would look at him. He wanted her to see the sincerity in his eyes. It had been over five years since they had spoken, and he had thought of her every day. "You didn't mean what you wrote?"

"I was only with Franklin to get over you! I don't care about you anymore! Get away from me! I *hate* you!" She closed her eyes tightly.

He leaned in close to the side of her face. She could feel his breath and smelled the familiar smell of a long day's worth of perspiration clinging to his uniform. "Please give me a chance," he pleaded as he attempted to place his cheek against hers.

She recoiled and leaned to her right to avoid him. "Nikolas! Let me go!"

Nikolas reluctantly released her and took a few steps back. She leaned against her car and covered her face with her hands. She could hear him putting his helmet on. She took a deep breath as he mounted his bike and started the engine.

As he pulled away, she uncovered her face and did her best not to look in his direction. Her car door was already open. She quickly got inside and felt a piece of paper crinkle from under her as she sat down. She pulled it out and opened it. As she read the words inside the paper, her eyes started to burn with tears. She thought of Edward. She then let an image of Franklin's smile slip in and out of her mind. She remembered her anger and forced herself not to cry.

7

After Collin Bennett's untimely departure as CEO of Corpotex Software, Edward was handed the reins of full command. He kept the same office he'd had before the promotion, allowing Deidra to take the larger office for herself. She left it, for the most part, the way Mr. Bennett had kept it. At times, Deidra had lunch there with Mr. Bennett's widow. Some of his awards were still mounted to the walls. Years of service recognized and then taken away. Betrayal. It only triggered more resentment inside of Deidra. Franklin's death was one thing, but getting rid of Collin was ... pointless.

Edward adjusted as best as he could to the dramatic changes. Still, he felt that his role at Corpotex was somewhat blurry. In reality, his position as the new CEO was a welcome transition for those who wanted him there and an awkward adjustment for those working under him. Although he worked in recent months to assure his senior management team that he was not going to take away from the vision Mr. Bennett previously had for the company, adding his own flair was going to be a challenge. He worked hard to dig through and understand exact percentages of capital allocations. He made it a point to stroll through the call center areas in order to shake hands and practice "blending in," as Deidra had put it.

Deidra had explained privately to shareholders that there was a culture at Corpotex that needed some caressing and that Edward was the right man for the job—and not just because Franklin Andrews had wanted it that way. Collin Bennett's murder was not going to ruin Corpotex. Deidra wouldn't let it. She believed in Edward.

Edward's world had certainly become more convoluted—his role at work was in a strange but parallel synchronicity to his role with The Society, but he was able to manage with the help of others. When he wasn't able to do something for someone, other people seemed to pop up out of the blue to do those things for him. When he wasn't going over something with a member of the Corpotex team, he was on the phone with racing investors, his collections team, or his staff of Society event coordinators. Taking over as head of The Society was a lot more involved than he would ever have envisioned. And, at times, he wondered why they had even allowed him to do it. He imagined that the money Franklin had deposited into his mother's bank account during the years of his upbringing made it look like he had been Franklin's secret son. It may have seemed logical to them that he had taken over The Society. It may have even appeared to those unseen rulers of the world that Franklin and Edward were close. But when he thought about it too much, he dismissed it all and figured that the powers that be probably didn't care and must have had some serious confidence in Deidra's ability to guide him through it smoothly. Without her, he would have ended up in pieces and tossed into a dumpster somewhere by now.

He certainly didn't feel more confident than he had before (when he was just a marketing guy), but he had learned to fake like he was. And recently, the decline in profits from the races made him feel as if he was hated. He was willing to do whatever it would take to turn his reputation around. He needed their confidence back. He needed to prove himself. Every part of the Race had grown on him. He understood the mood it created in these people. Their powerful lives and the pressures that came with them could be put on hold for an evening without the prying eyes of the public or the judgmental media. While they were attending a pre-race party or an after-party, they were not the heads of companies, rushing to meet multi-million dollar deadlines. They dressed in costumes. They were eager spectators. They were free.

"Mr. Bloodgood," Anthony called to him from the doorway of his office. "I made the calls and no one can find the man."

Edward looked up and tilted his head to the side, puzzled. "Hmmm. Can you get Deidra in here, please?"

"Of course, sir," Anthony replied.

As often as Edward reminded Anthony that he did not need to call him "sir," Anthony continued to ignore it. Edward still tried to get used to it but found it difficult. He just didn't feel much like the "sir" type. He felt more like the "hey, man" type. Even when Anthony told him at the house over a glass of wine that Franklin had once booked a flight to Austin just to watch young Edward perform as Renfield in the ninth-grade drama club play, he addressed him as a "sir" while he apologized for upsetting him.

"What's up, Boss?" Deidra asked. She strolled into his office ahead of Anthony and took a seat near the large desk. It was covered in paperwork and a mass of manila folders. Anthony closed the door behind him and took his place next to Deidra. They both looked at Edward expectantly.

"Well? What's the deal with this Vincent guy?" Edward asked. "Is he dead? I need to know what's up so I can find someone else. Fast."

Deidra looked up at Anthony and waited for a response.

"I called the jails and hospitals in Dallas and Fort Worth. They don't have him. The police department has no record of an arrest," he answered.

Edward looked at Deidra. "Johnny said Vinny had been arrested, right?"

"In *Dallas*?" she asked with a you-are-such-an-idiot smirk across her face. "He didn't say *where* he had been arrested. It could have been in Mexico for all we know."

"Dammit," Edward sighed in frustration.

"He could have been arrested anywhere," she reminded him. "And that whole arrest story could have been a lie. Johnny hates Vinny."

"Great," Edward replied.

"Who did you talk to with the Dallas PD?" she asked Anthony.

"Someone in admin."

"And you called County as well?" she asked.

"Yes."

She looked down and stared at her acrylic nails. They were set short because she hated to wear them long. She had insisted that they be filed down to a perfectly squared tip. She never wore them just before or during a race that she participated in, so they painfully reminded her that, at present, she was merely an organizer at best. She was a benched player in the game. "Maybe you should ask your new friend, Nik Vaughn, about him."

"Who?" Edward asked with an inquisitive brow.

Anthony's eyes bulged as he did everything he could to hold his tongue.

"Your new friend from the track. Nikolas," Deidra reminded him. "The blond white guy that pulled up on the motorcycle with the black guy, Andre." She spoke with a razored bite.

"Ohhh," Edward remembered suddenly. "Why would *he* know?"

"He's an ex-cop," she answered mordantly. "His friend Andre is Dallas PD."

"Why didn't you tell me?"

Deidra sat back and crossed her legs and arms. "Why would I?"

Edward blinked a few times, stunned by the acidic tone she had just used with him. Especially since she didn't use that tone with him much anymore. It was her voice of disrespect that she had used mostly in the beginning of their relationship. That was back when she had been forced into showing him those proverbial underworld ropes. And although her overall patience with him had grown after sharing some mutual life and death experiences together, she sometimes still used that same tone with him when she wanted to remind him that he was much stupider than she had remembered him to be.

"It would have been nice to know," he snapped in return.

"Well, sorry. I just figured that since you let those guys get involved, you knew all about them already. Where they worked, who they were associated with ..." Her words were crisp.

"I get it, Deidra," Edward said. "I let some people help us that I knew nothing about. Got it. Thanks. It's already done, so what's the big deal?" he asked, obviously upset with her.

"Nothing." She wouldn't look up at him.

"What's going on?" Edward asked Anthony.

"Nothing, sir," he responded before looking at Deidra to read her reaction. "He and Mr. Clement … Andre … worked for Mr. Andrews. On occasion. Gene had recommended them … back when Gene was sober and reliable … and alive, of course. Nik has a lot of law enforcement connections. He's like their leader."

Gene … the drugged-out cop. Another guy Franklin killed. "So Nik's not a cop anymore?"

"Nope," Deidra answered flippantly.

"Why not?"

"My guess is because he has to lay low now that he has a bigger role with the Knights. He's a chef now. Went to culinary school anyway before joining the PD," she explained. "Or maybe he just likes to cook instead. Maybe it pays more than the PD. I don't know. Don't care either."

"Oh." Edward studied Deidra. "Contact … him, Nikolas, for me and see what information he can help us get on Vincent."

"Nope."

Edward slammed his hand down on his desk and pursed his lips together. His face was now turning red. "Anthony," he grumbled.

"Yes, sir?"

"Please contact Nikolas for me."

"Of course, sir."

8

Deidra rushed around her apartment, frantically clean-ing. In one hand she held a fluffy duster and in the other a travel makeup bag. When her cell phone rang, she tossed the bag onto her coffee table and grabbed the phone from its resting place on the arm of the couch. "Hi, Eddie."

"What's going on with you? Are you still upset about your family ... uh ... situation?" he asked with care.

"I don't know. Maybe," she replied softly.

"I'm sure you think I was being rude to you earlier, but I have a responsibility to get this thing back together."

"I know that."

"You can't just expect me to sit back and take it when you push me like that. I care about you and this whole thing is awkward for me," he explained. "Being your boss is strange. It feels wrong."

She froze in place. "Are you firing me?"

"What? No!"

Deidra sat on her couch and waited for him to speak again. She was ready to get the conversation over with. She knew that in order for that to happen, she was going to have to let him say what it was that he wanted to say. She needed to finish packing so that she could be with her *abuelita*.

"I would like for you to come over," Edward said.

"Now?"

"Please."

"Eddie, I'm packing. I need to go to San Antonio for a few days."

Edward was silent.

"Is that okay?"

"Of course it is. Anything you need to do to take care of things with your grandmother is fine. I understand." Edward was upset for her. "Do you need me to arrange for someone to take you?"

"I booked a flight." Her voice cracked.

"Okay. Look, don't worry about anything going on here. Do what you need to do. If you need anything ..."

"Thanks."

He ended the call and slumped down in his seat. He missed her. He missed the laughs and the jokes. He missed her sarcasm and her sick sense of humor. She had been someplace else mentally for weeks, and it was killing him inside.

It was only a month ago that she had stayed the night in his lonely, oversized home. They sat up talking and looking up scenes from old movies on the Internet. They listened to music and drank until daylight. She fell asleep in an armchair as he watched over her. When the housekeeper got up to make his breakfast, he asked her not to. He didn't want a single sound to wake Deidra.

There was some noise downstairs and then, moments later, a knock at his bedroom door.

"Yes?"

"Sir," Malcolm, his live-in security guard, said through the door. "Sorry to bother you, but there is a man at the gate. He says it's very important that he speak to you."

"What's his name? Did he say?" Edward asked, pulling a pair of jeans out from a drawer. If he was about to talk to someone about anything serious, it wasn't going to be while he was in his Star Wars pajamas.

"Yes," Malcolm answered. "He says his name is Nikolas. Cameras showed him on a motorcycle."

"Let him in. I'll meet him in my office."

While Nikolas waited for Mr. Bloodgood, he checked the time on his phone and studied the statues positioned along the walls. Their blank eyes and upward stares made him feel uneasy. He knew some of them from art books, but he had only casually flipped through them out of complete boredom. The statues had previously belonged to Mr. Andrews, and Deidra had picked each one of them out specifically. There was some meaning in their design that she had never bothered to explain to him. She probably knew that he either wouldn't understand, or that he was too wrapped up in his own world to care.

"I'm surprised to see you here, Mr. Vaughn," Edward greeted Nikolas as he entered the office. "Can I get you anything to drink?"

"No, thank you, Mr. Bloodgood. I apologize for showing up like this, but a phone call wouldn't have been appropriate."

Edward motioned with his hand for Nikolas to take a seat and he obliged. Edward then sat next to him on the same side of the desk. It now looked like they were both waiting to speak to someone and not to each other.

"What's going on?" Edward asked.

Nikolas looked at the sleeve of his leather jacket and thought for a moment. "I don't really know how to put this," he began. "Anthony called me today and asked about Vincent Carracci."

"I've been looking for him. I was told he had been arrested recently."

"He was," Nikolas confirmed. "It was for speeding. Excessively. In a car with some illegal mods on it. He crashed."

"Oh," Edward replied. "So you guys *do* have him? I mean, the PD?"

Nikolas gazed at the rug beneath his chair. The patterns blurred as he tried to think of a way to tell the new man in charge that one of his racers was probably never coming back to racing. "These guys are easy to replace, right?" he asked with a half-joking type of a smile.

Edward frowned. "Well, according to Ms. Bonaparte, they are as easy to replace as a catalytic converter without the right ramp thing and something about bolts … I think she was trying to tell me that it was hard to replace these guys."

"That's not good."

"What happened? Is he dead?" Edward leaned forward in anticipation. The anxiety was already building up inside of him. The task of seeking out another racer that could be conditioned to keep quiet, fit an impossibly demanding profile, and be just insane enough—while not overly

psychotic—would be nerve-wracking. Contracts and reloca-
tions were involved. The man or woman recruited could not
be committed to a traditional family lifestyle. Deidra insisted
that, if they were to die in an accident, no children be left
without a parent as a result.

"He's not dead," Nikolas said slowly. "He's in a mental
institution."

Edward sat back a little, relieved. "Okay, I can deal with
that. Does he have a diagnosis yet? What happened?"

"Well, ... if there is a diagnosis, it's probably not official.
When they took him in, he was admitted as a John Doe."
Nikolas stopped so he could prepare himself to continue.
He scratched at a hole in his jeans before speaking again. "To
cover things up."

"What things?"

"They said he ... went crazy. Like ... possessed. Demon
stuff, I guess." Nikolas waited for a reaction.

"Okay, he went nuts. I'll look for someone else." Edward
leaned back and looked through Nikolas. He thought about
the application process Deidra had attempted to explain to
him the day before. Her explanation ended with the words,
"and that's why we get stuck with people like Johnny."

"No, I mean they are saying that he *is* possessed," Nikolas
stressed. "He's talking backward and ... things are levitating
around him. His eyes are turning in his head."

"I wish him the best and I hope he can get the medical
treatment he deserves, but—"

"He's talking about The Afterlife Society."

Edward froze.

"He's rambling and saying things that he shouldn't."

"Well, if he's really possessed, they won't know what he's talking about anyway," Edward suggested. "Right?"

Nikolas looked down at his hands and sighed. "Honestly, I think he should be taken care of."

"Isn't that why he's in the hospital?"

"No. I mean *killed*."

"Sorry, I'm still getting used to this." Edward picked up the phone on his desk. "I need to talk to someone about this first."

"Of course." Nikolas got up from his seat and reached out for Edward's hand. "Thank you for having me over, Mr. Bloodgood."

"Edward," he smiled while placing the receiver back down to accept the handshake. *The cell phone might be safer.*

"Thank you, Edward."

Nikolas opened the door and headed out as Edward followed close behind to walk with him to the foyer.

"Is there any way we could visit Mr. Carracci?" Edward asked.

"Uh, I'm not sure."

"Hmm."

"You don't believe me, do you?" Nikolas smiled and picked up his helmet from a table by the huge front doors. "About him being possessed."

"I don't know," Edward replied honestly. "I just don't believe in that kind of stuff. Never have."

"Well, neither do I." Nikolas shrugged his shoulders and then opened one of the front doors to leave. Before stepping out, he turned back and looked over Edward's shoulder to take in a quick parting view of the grand entrance. "I had a lot of respect for your father. He left you a nice place here."

Edward looked at him blankly and said nothing. In light of the conversation they had just had, the comment caught him off guard. In recent weeks, it had become clear to Edward that even after taking the time to explain his non-relationship with Franklin, people did not understand the situation anyway. No one but Deidra knew that Edward had been the one who shot Franklin. And as far as The Society knew, Franklin had committed suicide. Deidra explained to Edward that it was the right thing to do—and that, technically, it was true.

"Thank you," Edward replied with some discomfort. His eyes were downcast, staring at the floor.

"I'll get back to you about visiting Carracci."

"Thanks." Edward closed the door behind Nikolas as he left and immediately held up his cell phone to call Deidra. Images of scary movie scenes played through his head. It just didn't register with him. Demons, goblins, and ghouls could not share the same space with reality.

"Hey," she answered.

"That Vaughn guy was here."

"Why?" She sounded repulsed. Surprised and repulsed at the same time.

"He wanted to tell me that Vincent is in a mental hospital," Edward said. His tone reflected the surprise he felt when first hearing the news.

"Wow. Really?"

"That's what he said." He needed her input on the situation before taking the next step.

"He just showed up to tell you that?"

"Yes."

She didn't sound worried enough to him.

"At your house?" she asked.

"What's the problem?"

"The problem is that Nik is concerned about nothing but himself ... for the most part. He cares about his club and his job, but that's about it. Caring about Vinny 'the Snake' Carracci? I don't see it," she finished with a forced, short laugh.

"Is your line good?"

"Secure? Yeah. It always is. Yours should be too unless you've reset your phone."

"This is going to sound weird, but he said the PD had Vincent and that they committed him to a mental hospital."

Deidra gasped. "What the fuck for?!"

"This is the freaky part," he warned her. "For being ... *possessed.*"

Silence. It wasn't a silence he had expected either. It was a dead silence. One without a breath to be heard or a dropping of the phone from her hand.

"It's stupid, right?" Edward chuckled, but only to add something to that silence while he thought about what to say next. "So I asked Nikolas if I could visit with Vinny and he said he would see what he could do."

Still silence.

"Deidra?"

"Eddie," she took a few seconds to clear her throat. "That's bad."

"You believe it?"

"Well, it depends. I don't know the story, so how can I really know what's going on with him? Vincent is such a damn … he gets into so much trouble." She paused for a second to get her thoughts back on track. "I would have to do an evaluation of him myself. There are ways you can tell. I need to know how he's been acting … behavioral patterns. I need to know how he's been eating and sleeping."

She paused again.

"I need to hear his voice," she told him.

"This is crazy." Edward closed his eyes and raised his hand into the air. He clenched his jaw tight. "Will you come to the hospital with me to see him then?"

"Edward!" she snapped. "I can't! I'm going to San Antonio to see my grandmother! My father and my brother are waiting for me."

"Well, how am I going to know what to do about Vincent?"

"I don't know. Take Anthony. He's seen some messed up stuff over the years," she offered as a suggestion. "Besides, possession cases are rare. Most turn out to be mental illness. The theories on it are endless. It could be that parts of the brain are temporarily activated that we don't understand … causing, like, a telekinetic response."

"Uh …" Edward looked down at the variety of cream-colored patterns on the floor, barely understanding a word she had said. "Yeah, he probably just hit his head. It was a car crash."

"Exactly," she agreed.

"I need to get this race organized quickly, and I have angry investors watching my every move, and a mentally ill racer that I need to replace or rescue from a hospital because some chef-biker-cop guy says he's saying crazy things about us—"

"It will be okay. You have two guys who already agreed to race. Focus on them, get the next cars ready, prep your mechanics, then go see Vinny when you have time. I hate to let him sit and rot in some hospital, but for now, you have other priorities."

He knew she was right. "Yeah. Be safe on your trip."

"I'm leaving in the morning and I'll be back in about three days, I think." She studied several pairs of shoes she had lined up on the floor of her large, walk-in closet. "Try to relax. Vincent has even more drama issues than Johnny. I'm sure it's just a case of asshole-itis."

9

San Antonio was just the same as she had left it. Amazingly beautiful. Grotesquely hot, humid, and about 103 degrees, but amazing just the same. The buildings were still as culturally rich as she had remembered, and the people were just as interesting.

Her father picked her up from the airport and then took her straight to a hospital in the downtown area where her grandmother had been admitted.

"She is only speaking Spanish today," he told her, with his eyes still on the road. "I don't know why." He smiled.

They parked his rental car and sat for a moment with the engine still running. Her father had always reminded her of Bela Lugosi for some reason. He was half Spanish-Mexican and half French with naturally black hair that he now tried to keep dark even as he aged out of it. He had a seriousness about him that intimidated many. He could often be seen standing still, in deep thought, looking like the type of old photo taken before people were forced to smile in them. So as a child, when she flipped through one of her brother's books about horror movies and discovered a famous photo of Lugosi, every part of his striking face, including the eerie expression captured, reminded her of her father.

"Your brother is up there in the room with her," he said, pointing up toward a tall section of the hospital before them. "Try not to fight with him in front of her."

"I won't," she assured him.

"He's going through a lot."

"Like what?" she asked, doing her best not to put too much sarcasm into her words.

Her father squinted his eyes and ran his fingers across the steering wheel. It was obvious to Deidra that he was stalling. "He requested some time off."

She thought for a moment before giving up and asking, "What for?"

"He doesn't want to practice any longer. At least, not for the Church," he explained to her. She could tell that he was trying to hide the disappointment in his voice.

"He's excommunicating himself?"

"In a way, yes." He looked at her for a reaction. "But don't put it like that to him. He was already having a hard time with some of the policies, and then ... something happened recently that pushed him in this direction."

"Dad," she began in a deepened tone. "He drinks, he curses incessantly, he gets into bar fights, and he's pulled a gun on a guy. He was never priest material."

"He is devoutly religious, Deidra. He's the most spiritual man I know."

"He flirts with women," she smiled. "I've seen it."

Her father checked his collar and turned off the car. "Remember not to mention it to him. And remember that your *abuelita* is very proud of him for his work with the Church."

"Okay, okay. Has he done that thing yet where he corrects how people pronounce his name? 'It's not Martin, it's Marteeeen!'"

Her father let out a light giggle. "Yes. Twice."

"El es muy guapo, Martin. Mi amor." His grandmother touched his cheek gently from her hospital bed.

Martin smiled and touched her arm. *"Gracias, Abuelita."*

He stood when he saw his father at the doorway with Deidra. Martin was over six feet tall by five inches, and muscular-looking in his fitted t-shirt. His jeans hung loose and had some wear in them. "I will be right back," he said gently to his grandmother.

Martin walked out of the room to greet his sister but felt hesitant to follow through. She stood rigid and stared at him with doubt in her eyes. Doubt that he believed stemmed from their last turbulent visit.

Their father decided at that moment that he should speak about anything to break the tension between them. "Your sister's flight was nice and smooth, right, Deidra?" He then looked at her expectantly, hoping that she would take the opportunity to reconnect with her brother.

"Where's Pablo, Christian, and Mike?" she asked, looking through Martin as she spoke.

"Christian is trying to get here tomorrow and Pablo is still out of the country, in Italy," her father reminded her. "Don't you remember?"

"And Mike?"

"How are you, Deidra?" Martin asked.

Deidra looked at him with a disgusted expression across her face. "Hello."

"How is work going?" Martin's tone was one of extreme caution and forced pleasantry. He was going to be the bigger person now and do what he could to make her see that he wanted to set their differences aside.

"Fine," she replied, disinterested in his attempt to wave the white flag.

"How's Frank?"

"He *died*." She scowled at him.

Martin tried not to appear shocked at the coolness of her voice. He scanned his memory for a moment, trying to recall if he had missed something about Franklin's passing. "Sorry."

"What's up with you?" she tilted her hip and placed a hand on her waist. She was making it obvious to him that she already knew something was up. She looked at the small crucifix handing from his neck.

"Not much." He looked around anxiously.

Their father reached out to touch each of them on the shoulder. "Let's go in and see how grandma's doing, okay? She will be so happy to see you both together."

"We don't normally do this, Mr. Bloodgood. Our facility is very careful about security, and we take our policies very seriously." The man in the suit was unlocking the door they were standing in front of. Edward had been told in a phone call that morning to ask for Dr. Armstrong at the front desk. The doctor met him in the lobby and quickly rushed him up a flight of stairs.

"He's been in here for two nights," the doctor said as they continued walking in a hurried fashion down a long hallway. It was lit by florescent lights that were either too dim or flickering. The doctor's hair was messy and flattened in the back. He appeared to have been awoken by Edward's arrival. As he continued to follow the doctor down the hall, Edward noticed that the quickness of his pace was now slowing. The doctor's hands were shaking erratically and his face looked very panicked and uneasy. "Sorry about the request, sir. Five minutes is all I can give you once we get in to see him."

"I understand. I appreciate your help," Edward answered in return.

"Anything for the Knights, sir. They told me you were ... *are* important. They've helped us out in the past." As they reached the end of the hallway, the doctor stopped to fumble through his pockets. He pulled out a piece of paper and typed in some numbers on a keypad attached to the wall next to the door.

He paused and looked back at Edward nervously.

"Are you okay?" Edward asked. The expression on the doctor's face was set like marble. The stiffness of his lips and brow sent a chill through Edward's body.

"Yes. I'm supposed to have this code memorized. They don't change it too often," he mumbled. "They lie and say that they do, though."

"Oh." Edward knew that the man had his mind on something other than the damn code. He was having second thoughts.

The door clicked and then opened. They went through only to end up inside another hallway. The only light came from a dusty window that glowed at the end of the narrow, dank hall. A security guard stood in front of a door at the end.

"He's in there. We have to hurry," the doctor warned him.

"Has he been diagnosed with anything?" Edward remembered to ask.

"Hold on a second," the doctor requested with his hand held up. They stopped in front of the security guard. "I need to see the patient for a few minutes."

"Yes, sir." The guard opened the door and stepped aside. He watched Edward with wide eyes as he followed the disheveled doctor into the darkened room.

"No. He hasn't been diagnosed yet because, well ... look at him." The doctor shivered and held his hand outward, motioning toward a man strapped to a hospital bed, surrounded by a mist of cold air. The man's eyes looked huge, as if held open by some unseen force. He was staring at the ceiling and seemed to be looking through a single pen that was levitated above his head, spinning slowly in place.

"Whoa," Edward hugged the sides of his body and tensed his muscles. The temperature in the room was extremely cold.

The doctor took a step backward and cleared his throat quietly. "We want to get a priest in here as soon as possible, but we haven't had to deal with a case like this before. And I wasn't sure what to do, because I was told by Officer Clement that Mr. Carracci was connected to some government stuff and to be careful not to bring any attention to him." The doctor paused uncomfortably before explaining further. "The patient has been rambling about some ... secret society."

Ronnie Stich

"Okay," Edward said in a tone that gave the doctor a cue to stop before he said something that he shouldn't. He continued to stare at the spinning pen hovering a foot above Vincent's face.

"I'm glad you're here, Mr. Bloodgood. I was hoping someone would come in and tell me what I can do with him."

"Well," Edward raised his eyebrows and watched as Vincent turned his pale, bluish face toward the sound of his voice. "I need to get a few of our people in here—"

"And a priest?" the doctor asked quickly.

"Uh, yeah. I guess I can work that out," Edward said, sure that someplace in their network of professionals and secret operative connections, there had to be some form of a church connection amongst them. Not that he was confident that one might help them.

"Mr. Bloodgood, I can't keep this quiet for much longer."

Vincent opened his mouth and licked his cracked, dry lips. The pen fell suddenly and grazed the side of his head.

"I need to make a phone call. Can I take a picture of him with my phone first?" Edward asked. "You know ... so I can get you some help."

"I guess so. I just don't want it getting out somehow or ending up connected to this facility," the doctor said anxiously.

"Of course. You have my word."

Edward took a few steps toward Vincent's bed. With only about five feet between them, he could clearly make out the bloody cracks on his lips and the excessive amount of oil in his dark hair. "Vincent, my name is Edward."

Vincent responded by groaning deeply. The throatiness of it was unnatural—what Edward would have expected to

70

hear from a decaying zombie dragging itself across a grave-yard on the set of a movie.

"I'm here to ask if you would like to come back to drive for us. I took over for Mr. Andrews."

Vincent's eyes shifted back and forth at an abnormally fast speed. They appeared to roll back and shake beneath his eyelids. "Franklin says your mom was insatiable." He then laughed deeply and growled. This time, the noise was animal-like and primal.

Edward held his phone up and moved in a foot closer. He swallowed hard and then captured a steady enough photo before asking, "Can you talk to Franklin?"

Vincent stopped growling and his face froze, contorted into place. His mouth was open wide, and his tongue vibrated at a speed that seemed impossible.

"Tell me what Franklin is up to," Edward asked.

The doctor cautiously observed and tilted his body for a better view.

Vincent convulsed violently. The straps of leather that were holding him down creaked. His body suddenly went still and his hands twitched. "He said to tell you that you fucked up his bedroom. PUT BACK THE OLD CURTAINS!" he screamed.

Edward took another photo as the screaming continued. Vincent writhed from underneath the straps, flipping his head back and forth hard against the pillowless mattress. His bony, claw-like hands now gripped the sides of the bed.

"Mr. Bloodgood, we have to go," Dr. Armstrong reminded him.

"Hey, Vincent," Edward said, bending down enough to get a profile picture. "Jesus loves you."

Vincent screeched in agony, his back arched, and the bed began to shake. The headboard repeatedly slammed against the wall. His eyes fluttered and spun unnaturally as his head turned from left to right as fast as it could handle.

Edward was holding his phone steady as he stepped backwards so that the video he was filming would be clear when he showed it to Deidra.

10

"I'm in a hospital cafeteria," she texted back to Edward. "WTF is going on?"

Martin and her father sat across from her. They were discussing treatment options and other medical things she didn't want to think about when it came to her grandmother—the woman who had taken care of her when her own mother would go to evening classes and her father would be away on a government assignment. As her father sat with good posture and ate with eloquent manners, her brother irritated her as he did just the opposite. He chewed loudly and hunched over his cafeteria tray much like she imagined a sasquatch might.

Edward texted her again. "Vincent IS POSSESSED!" it read.

She looked at her father and lowered the phone down from the table and placed it on her lap to text back, "U saw?"

Almost immediately he sent back, "Yes!"

She stared at the phone, puzzled.

Then a message came in with an attachment. It was a photo. She debated between opening it at the table or excusing herself to go pretend to use the bathroom. Impatience got the best of her. She clicked on it.

"Holy Jesus!" she yelped, before catching herself.

Martin dropped the biscuit from his hand onto the table with a start. "What's wrong?" her brother asked with too much food in his mouth.

She looked up and smiled. "Nothing."

Another text then followed. It read, "They want a priest. What do I do?"

She looked up from her lap with only her eyes. She scanned her brother over. His messy-on-purpose black hair and heavy cologne aggravated her. The musky smell had overpowered their table and ruined the flavor of her tater tots. "Will call you in a few mins," she replied to Edward.

"Martin," she said across the table, inconspicuously. "Can I speak to you for a few minutes before we go back up to the room?"

"Sure," he agreed while slurping soup from a plastic spoon.

Her father smiled proudly, believing that she was making an effort. "I need a coffee. I will leave you two to talk for a bit."

"No, Dad," Deidra pleaded weakly.

"Talk to each other." He continued to smile and stood to walk towards the front of the cafeteria.

Deidra placed her phone on the table. She pushed her tray away and set her elbows down in front of her. Some of the bracelets on her arm jingled as she folded her hands together. "I might need your help."

"Really?" Martin stopped slurping to listen.

"Yes." Her phone rang and she pressed the reject button. "I need you to go to Dallas with me."

"For what?" His face crinkled.

She glanced over Martin's shoulder to check on her father's progress with his coffee. And her father was watching her in return.

"Look at this," she said, snatching her phone from the table and scanning through the last few messages she'd received. She opened the photo of Vincent and zoomed in enough to make the disturbing expressions on his face appear in sharper detail. She held out her phone and watched for a reaction from her eldest brother.

Martin leaned in, only looking at the picture for a few seconds before pushing himself back from the table. He appeared unaffected and even somewhat dismissive in his reaction. "Is this a joke?"

"A *joke*?" she stressed, insulted at the mere suggestion of it.

"Yes. To *mock* me? I'm sure dad told you that I am leaving the Church. Well, guess what? I only told him that to make him feel better! Because of what happened to Mom when *she* was threatened!" He eyed her furiously and pointed a shaky finger at her phone. "They threatened my life again! Those … fanatics! Over *that kind of stuff!* Because I help people!"

"Martin! Lower your voice."

"You don't care! Have you ever cared about anything I have done to serve Our Lord and Savior?"

"Martin! I am asking you for your help!" She locked her phone and shoved it inside her handbag. "Never-fucking-mind!"

She stood up and shoved her seat backward, almost tipping it over in the process. It scraped loudly against the floor and caused her father to grimace with embarrassment. She turned to make her way out of the cafeteria. "Never mind. I'll find another damn priest. A *real* one."

"What did you just say?" Martin asked as he slowly stood.

Deidra turned back and looked him over disapprovingly. "I asked you for help and you treated it as if it was a joke. A real priest helps people when they ask for help, don't they?"

"Where did you get that picture? The Internet?" he asked defensively. "You knew, didn't you?! That I had a death threat recently and that I've been in hiding … because of stuff like that!"

"No. It was sent to me in a text message!" she yelled. "From a hospital in Dallas!"

Her father stopped stirring the hydrogenated creamer that he would never normally use in his coffee, set his cup down quickly, and walked hastily toward the section of the long rectangular table that his grown children were arguing at. Almost every person dining in the cafeteria was gawking at them, most having assumed that they were a sweet-looking couple until the man started yelling about being a priest to the woman who was all tensed up and ready to storm out of the room.

To the enjoyment of those watching, Deidra then grabbed a handful of tater tots.

"Are you going to *throw* those at me?" her brother asked in his deepest, most threatening voice.

"Do you want me to?"

"I *dare* you."

Deidra's father glanced around the room as his pace quickened. He was doing his best to avoid eye contact with any of the strangers watching him. It was obvious that everyone in the room was waiting for the crazed woman to launch some tots at the man standing across the table from her.

"See what you did?! Now Dad's coming!" she hissed. "This is your fault!"

"What are you two doing?!" her father asked. He was red with embarrassment. "Martin! Sit down! Deidra—"

"I'm going to see Grandma and then I have to go," she said to her father while doing her best to compose herself. "I'm sorry. Something is going on and I have to get back to Dallas."

She popped a tater tot into her mouth and turned abruptly to leave.

11

Edward played the video again on his laptop. He could barely stomach the look in Vincent's eyes. It disturbed him in a way that he could not have imagined. He spent an hour searching videos online to compare it to but thought that most of them looked fake. The few that he did find to be convincing enough were also too horrific for him to believe. They were extreme and too graphic. They just couldn't be real. His was genuine. He was there when it happened.

He remembered the pair of headphones he had in the drawer of his desk. After shuffling through the drawer and opening and closing a few others in haste, he found the headphones already plugged into the laptop. He reset the video to play from the beginning and listened closely. He leaned in to the screen, mesmerized with the phenomenon he had captured, and tuned into the variations in the groans and growls. Then something within the audio playback caused him to sit up with a jolt.

"What the hell?" He clicked on the right spot to play back the last ten seconds. "Oh my God."

He reached instinctively for his phone. But then he remembered not to bother Deidra. He held his arm frozen over the cell phone in thought. And before Edward could look back to the computer screen again, his phone vibrated on the desk. It was a text message.

It read, "I hate my bro :(."

He frowned and texted back, "I'm sorry. Is ur gma ok?" "Blah."

"When r u coming back?" he sent.

He waited about fifteen seconds before she replied, "I'm in ur kitchen. Why don't u have wine???"

Edward smiled and shook his head.

"R u looking in the wine room down the hall from u? Grab a bottle and a few glasses. Meet me in office up stores." He reread what he had sent and then corrected himself. "Upstairs."

As he waited, he refreshed and replayed the video, watching and listening to it again in its entirety. What he couldn't seem to shake was the fear he had built up inside him. With each viewing, it didn't become less daunting—it became worse. The reality of it was bad enough. And the possibilities of what was to come by investigating it further could be a lot more sinister than he was prepared for.

The sound of footsteps coming up the stairs became louder, and he removed his headphones. Edward waited for the door to open, but there was a knock instead.

"You can come in, Deidra. You don't have to knock," he said sarcastically. "Wait until you see this video."

He looked up and was surprised to see Nikolas standing in the doorway.

"Hi," Nikolas greeted him. "Sorry, but Deidra let me in and told me I could come up here."

"Oh," Edward replied. "That's okay. I was just ... not ... expecting you."

Nikolas smiled and looked down. "Well, I didn't expect to be here either. I don't plan to drop in like this uninvited all the time. I promise. But, I heard about your visit to the hospital today and I …"

Edward glanced at the screen of his laptop and then back at Nikolas. "Yes, thank you for helping me get in there." He smiled sincerely, also hoping that the drop-ins would not become a regular thing.

"No problem. We've helped them with a few undesirables." Nikolas stepped further into the room and began to close the door behind him as Deidra pushed it open with excessive force, knowing that Nikolas was standing there. The door hit him with a hard thud against the shoulders, and he moved aside with a grimace on his face.

"Excuse me," he said to her meekly as she passed him.

"I picked a red. It's not a super oaky one, though, so you should like it," she said to Edward as she placed two wine glasses on the desk. She plunked down into a large leather chair, still holding the wine bottle in her hands. She was eager to pour it.

Edward looked behind her to read the expression on Nikolas's face. Nikolas smiled smoothly in return and instead of taking the available seat next to Deidra, he stepped backward and off to his left a bit to lean against the wall. He crossed his arms and legs. The leather of his jacket squeaked.

"I think I have an extra glass here in my little bar area." Edward rolled his chair across the floor and reached over to his right to open a cabinet filled with liquor and assorted tumblers. Most of the bottles had never been opened and sat neglected underneath a light coating of dust.

"You don't need to worry about me, sir," Nikolas said as he nodded once in a show of appreciation.

"He hates red wine anyway." Deidra could not hide the irritation creeping through in her voice.

"I have been learning to appreciate it, actually," Nikolas corrected her. "People change."

Edward stopped staring into the wood cabinet off to the side of his desk. He pushed himself back in front of his laptop and put on a fake smile. "I think Mr. Vaughn can speak for himself," he said slowly, in an attempt to remind her of her manners in front of their guest.

Nikolas pushed out a forceful breath through his nostrils and smirked. Although he stood there putting on his best portrayal of a man unaffected, his heart had been pierced and damaged by Deidra. It had taken over two years for him to work up enough courage to talk to her again—and mere seconds for her to tear him back down. Standing in the same room with her was very difficult. "It's okay. I don't plan on staying very long." Nikolas cleared his throat. "I was told that you got a good look at Vincent this afternoon."

"Yes!" Edward replied excitedly while watching Deidra set the wine bottle on the end of the desk. She unfolded a wine key he recognized from a drawer in his kitchen. "The doctor that let me in was very nice. He said your club had helped him in the past. He seemed eager to pay back the favor."

Deidra stopped twisting the mysterious metal spiral that Edward had never learned to use and let out a shaky sigh. "You guys still do that stuff?" she asked without looking back toward Nikolas.

Nikolas tilted his head to the side, as if attempting to look around the back of her head to stare into her face. "Of course we do." His delivery was stern.

"Do what?" Edward asked. He was tired of being in the dark about things.

Nikolas looked at Edward and remained silent. Deidra did the same.

"Well?" Edward pressed them.

"We help take care of violent criminals that the justice system can't. Too many loopholes in the law," Nikolas answered. "I only helped Danny ... Dr. Armstrong, a few times. He's a good guy."

Edward set his elbows on the desk and rested his chin in his hands. His eyes were vacant for a moment and then filled with admiration when he realized what was being said. "Well, that's good, right? I mean ... you *kill* criminals?"

"Yes," Deidra answered quietly. She then returned her attention to the wine bottle and started twisting the key deeper into the cork. "They have taken care of some pretty disgusting people. Rapists, child killers ... all of them would have gotten away with it somehow without the network of law enforcement and other professionals they know. The Secular Knights."

"Wow. That takes a lot of guts," Edward praised him.

Nikolas nodded gracefully and looked at the back of Deidra's head. "Thanks."

Edward smiled half-heartedly as he thought about it further. He was confused now, not knowing whether he viewed Nikolas more as a gourmet chef or as a rebel ex-lawman carrying out a vendetta against society's most intolerable scumbags. He wondered if Nikolas carried out the killings himself or if he had some of his club members do them for him.

"What did you think of Vincent?" Nikolas asked, interrupting Edward's thoughts.

Edward paused a moment before answering. "I think the police department was right. He seems possessed."

"Well, yes," Deidra began. "It *seems* that way, but we need an expert to get in there and make the final assessment."

"Are we going to do that?" Edward asked his question openly to both of them.

"Deidra's brother is a priest," Nikolas told him.

"What the fuck is wrong with you?" Deidra stood up from her seat and turned to glare at Nikolas. "Is that really your business?"

"It's public knowledge," he replied.

"Are you volunteering my brother for this shit? Do you even care how the Church would react to him getting involved?" Her hands were shaking … with guilt.

"Wait," Edward stopped them with his hands in the air before him. "The brother in San Antonio?"

"Yes," she snapped, still focused on Nikolas.

"Can he at least come and evaluate him?"

"No!" she said adamantly. "He's a fucking jerk and he's all screwed up in the head." She turned back to Edward. "I think he's … going through a lot right now and doesn't want to get involved in this kind of thing."

"Why?" Edward asked.

"What does it matter?!" she yelled. "I showed him the picture you sent! He thought it was a fake and treated me like crap over it."

"What if you showed him a video?" Edward offered.

Nikolas took a step forward. "The Church never stopped him before when he did all those other jobs. What if I talk to him?"

Deidra spun around and pointed at him. "Don't you dare call *my* brother. Stay out of it."

"Calm down," Edward said. "Let's just find someone locally instead or ask our government guys to suggest someone."

"Her brother has performed exorcisms before," Nikolas informed him. "He has done a few for the government. He's seen a lot of things and is very good at what he does. If you asked the government for someone, they'd probably recommend *him*."

"What kind of exorcisms does the government usually get involved with?" Edward asked. The idea creeped him out.

"You don't hear about it much because you're not supposed to," Deidra said with indifference and a sip of her wine. "There have been a few cases involving teenagers. You know ... politicians' kids."

"Really?" Edward was stunned.

She looked away from Edward and into the beverage in her hand. As much as she tried to keep her composure, she lost it when she forced the entire glass of wine down at once and tensed her shoulders. Her eyes watered. "Ask him why he thinks he's so close to my brother."

Edward looked at Nikolas. He watched him uncross his arms and shuffle his feet before settling into a new spot to lean on against the wall. "Are you good friends with her brother?"

"Yes," he answered.

"Why?" Edward wasn't really sure he wanted to know.

Nikolas stared at the back of Deidra's head. "Because I met him on a trip to San Antonio."

Deidra grimaced. "He knows my dad, too."

Edward's face took on a look of confusion mixed with horror. The more he learned about Nik Vaughn, the more he wondered why Deidra had never mentioned him before.

"I kept in touch with him, with Martin, because of a job we both ended up working on together," Nikolas said in his own defense. He could see that Edward's reaction was not good. He was aware of how much time Edward spent with Deidra. He saw them together a lot around town. He also wasn't blind to Edward's admiration for her. But Edward didn't come off as threatening as Franklin had been.

Deidra's hands were shaking. "You need to stay away from my family. I don't want my brother helping us. Martin isn't doing jobs for the government anymore. He's too conflicted right now and he needs a break," she said, turning to Edward as if pleading with him. "And I hate him!"

Edward shook himself from the disbelief he was experiencing. "Um ... wait ... so why does Mr. Vaughn know your dad?"

"Come on, Eddie," she answered. "It was before I worked for Franklin. It doesn't matter anyway because it was all fake!"

"What was fake about it?" Nikolas asked.

"All of it." She turned to him. "You made that very clear when you ran away like a child."

Nikolas tensed. "Ran away? I was trying to survive! I could have been killed by that psycho! I have a commitment to society. I took an oath to protect and—"

"You're not a fucking cop anymore! Get over yourself! You proved that you will do whatever it takes to serve and protect *yourself* already!" she yelled.

"Sorry I called your dad a psycho," Nikolas quickly turned towards Edward and then back to Deidra. "An oath is an oath and I still serve. I serve society more now than I was ever able to on the force."

"Yeah ... uh ..." Edward managed to sputter out. "He was not my *dad*-dad. He was like ... my mom's stalker, kind of."

"Whatever!" Deidra yelled. She poured and drank another glass of wine as both men watched silently. When she was finished, she took a deep breath and looked at Edward with sadness in her eyes. "Can I pour you a glass?"

Edward swallowed back his discomfort and studied her trembling body. He set aside his own distaste with the awkwardness of their situation. "Sure."

She relaxed her shoulders and reached for his glass. She poured the wine with care and watched the expression on his face as she placed the glass down gently in front of him. "Maybe we should get back to this issue with Vinny?" she suggested.

"Are you willing to try talking your brother into helping us with this again?" Edward asked.

"I'll help get him out here," she replied.

Edward took a sip of his wine and motioned for Nikolas to take the other seat near his desk. "Come and sit down. I have a video you should both see. I just listened to a part that sounded like two voices coming out of Vincent's mouth at once."

He turned his laptop so that it faced the two chairs in front of his desk, and Deidra calmly sat back into her seat. She wasn't normally embarrassed by the things she said to or in front of anyone, but this time she was. She needed to set her past with Nikolas aside to focus herself forward in life.

"You can talk to Martin, Nik." She needed to invite him to help them in order to prove to herself that it didn't have a hold of her—old feelings of abandonment. There were questions unanswered that she just could not ask of him. He ran out of her life at the wrong time. Learning to work with him again would be therapeutic in a way. Or painfully traumatic.

"Are you sure that's okay with you?" Nikolas asked sheepishly.

"Yeah. He won't listen to me anyway."

Nikolas walked over to accept the vacant seat Edward had offered him. As he sat down, he couldn't help but notice the charm bracelet Deidra was wearing. It shined and captured the light coming from the lamp on her side of the desk. As Edward asked Deidra to press the play button on the screen with the touchpad, some of the charms hit the edge of the desk, making tiny thud sounds and they sparkled and danced in fast, jerky motions. Nikolas focused in on one charm in particular as it swung back and forth beneath her slender wrist. It was a sterling silver angel that she'd received just days before her 36th birthday and just hours after he shot the man who had killed her angelic mother. He purchased it for her after ridding himself of the man's body in the Rio Grande ... just as his future father-in-law had instructed him to.

If I had proposed, Frank would have killed me.

And even as he watched Vincent screaming in unholy agony on the screen in front of him, Nikolas couldn't help but wonder, in a hypnotic distraction, why she still wore the charm he had given her three long years ago.

12

"It's a long drive but you know I can't stand flying," Congressman Montemayor said into his cell phone. He swept back some of the dark hair from his forehead. "Plus I can bring along a few people this way. I'd like to stop at a few of the smaller towns also."

One of his assistants entered with a document and placed it quietly on top of his desk.

"Hold on a second," he said, pulling the phone away from his ear. He smiled at the young man in his office. "Is that the schedule for the awards ceremony thing?"

"Yes, sir," the assistant replied cheerfully.

"Okay, great. Can you take a seat for just a minute?" Congressman Montemayor motioned toward the chair in front of his desk and promptly returned to his phone call. "I need to call you back. Is that all right, Jess? Thanks … uh huh … bye bye."

The assistant took a seat in front of the large desk. It was covered in paperwork and always had a few coffee mugs scattered about. The mugs annoyed the assistant because Mr. Montemayor always seemed to place them on top of papers that he would then need to have reprinted. He wished that Mr. Montemayor could just use the same mug throughout the day, but unfortunately, his habit of drinking different flavors of coffee at the same time made that impossible. It also made him loathe those single-cup brewing machines with a passion.

"I'm trying to finalize some things before we get on the road next week," the congressman said as he folded a piece of paper on his desk. "Did we get that SUV rental I was hoping for?"

"Yes, sir. Tinted windows and plenty of room for luggage."

"Good job, Paul. I don't want anyone to think I'm paranoid or goin' loco, you know?"

"Yes, sir."

"But I know I would feel safer with some security taggin' along," he said with disappointment. "It's a damned shame that people have to go and ruin something as sacred as one's sense of personal safety."

His assistant looked down at his own fingers as he tapped the tips of them against the edge of the desk. "Because of the threat, sir?"

"Well, yes, of course." The congressman abruptly straightened up in his seat and glanced at the door to his office before speaking further. "That email was disturbing. Now, I don't scare too easily. I'm a rational man. Born and raised in this state ... I believe in the right to bear arms ... just never got around to buyin' any. I already got this good guy I know coming with us. He's an ex-cop. His uncle's a good friend of mine. His uncle's Chase Vaughn. You remember him? He helped fund a great deal of our campaign. ... Trustworthy family. But I'm still tryin' to contact some people and find a professional bodyguard to travel with us. And a good driver, too. One that looks scary."

"Sir," the assistant looked at him cautiously before continuing. "The only problem is that if we have you meeting with constituents and there's a couple of ... uh ... scary bodyguards around, it doesn't look very people-friendly."

"Hmmm." The congressman patted his protruding belly in contemplation. "I haven't hired anybody just yet. This guy Nik ... he's not too scary-lookin' when he's in plain clothes. He's got that biker thing goin' on ... I'll tell him to blend in. He's known to be a good shot, though, I'll tell you that much. Good with a knife, too."

"People aren't going to know about the email. They won't understand why you have those kinds of people around you. It might look a little egocentric."

Fernando thought about it for a moment and placed a finger on his mouth, brushing it along the edge of his lip. He tried to picture shaking hands with the men, women, and children that supported him as two armed guards stood nearby. He imagined being immersed in each community, learning about their issues and struggles, as armed men kept a dutiful watch. Paul was probably right. It would look intimidating, perhaps even unsettling to some, but his personal safety was at risk. There was more to this situation than Paul knew or could ever understand. The email meant nothing. He received emails like that all the time. It was the aliens that were really after him. That night at the lake haunted his memories—what little memory he had of it. He was either going to have protection or cancel the entire trip.

"Fuck it, Paul. I'm bringing at least one security guy for sure. We'll just have to figure out a way to make it look right."

"Phillip, sir."

"Who's that?" The congressman asked, leaning forward. Phillip smiled tolerantly.

"Sorry, Phillip. God damn. You know I'd lose my head too, son." The congressman pointed to his head and slumped over on his desk with a frown. "It's all scrambled up in here, Phillip. I just don't know what's wrong with me."

13

Edward stood outside his Mercedes with his body turned away from the bar behind him. His suit jacket was beginning to feel warm in the night's humidity. He hesitated to remove it in front of the group of bikers hanging around nearby. Their eyes studied him. Edward hoped that Deidra would show up quickly. He was certain that he looked like a moron and that his moron points were increasing by the minute. Deidra's edgy look and personality would help him blend in. He was the kind of guy who didn't belong in front of, inside of, or anyplace close to, a bar associated with bikers—even accidentally. Especially if by accident, in fact.

A sleek-looking classic car pulled up, interrupting Edward's self-abusive analysis of himself and his choice in clothing. The tires of the car caused a cloud of dirt to envelope its sides as the car parked several feet away from him. It was a black 1969 Camaro. Deidra stepped out in tall, black leather boots. Her jeans were fitted and had holes in them that were, no doubt, strategically placed there by some pricy designer. Edward held out his hands and shrugged his shoulders as he walked toward her.

"Where did you get that car, and why are you parked over here in the dirt?" Edward asked her.

"I found it and because I saw you in that stupid suit." She straightened out her black shirt and placed her handbag onto her arm. He once asked her about that bag in particular, wondering where he might get one like it for his mother because his next visit to Austin was coming up soon. Deidra had told him, "You can't pick out a Gucci *anything* for a girl. You have to know exactly what she wants." Then she'd said, "Get her a gift card instead. Let her pick it out." She also told him to be sure that he made the card for at least two thousand dollars. Later that day Edward found a gift card from Gucci sitting on his desk.

"I was in a meeting at work," he explained.

"You could have had Anthony bring you another outfit from the house," she suggested.

Edward pressed his lips together in frustration. "Yeah, I know. It's too late now, so let's just get this over with." He glanced around at the collection of motorcycles parked around them. He could hear the sound of animated voices in conversation over the heavy rock music playing from inside the bar they were about to enter. "I feel like an idiot."

She stood close to him and hooked her arm around his. "Don't worry. I was just messing with you," she said as she steered him closer to the entrance. "Did you forget that you run the show here?"

Edward smiled shyly. "Yes."

"I know these guys and how they operate. Just let me lead you through it when you get stuck, okay?"

"Okay."

She stepped with him through the entrance with her left arm wrapped tightly around his. They were hip to hip. It eased Edward's nerves to have her there to advise and lead him through conversations he still wasn't used to having. And it didn't hurt that Deidra's body was against his at the moment. If he hadn't been as nervous as he was, he might have enjoyed it a bit more.

The attention his suit received as they walked through the room was nothing compared to the attention Deidra drew to them. Some of the bikers gathered around the bar and stopped mid-beer guzzle to gawk at them, confused by the seemingly mismatched pair in their midst. Others openly laughed at Edward's suit and tie ensemble until they were elbowed or hushed by another one of their own. It only took a glance at the expression on Nikolas's face to know that the man in the suit was a welcomed guest. Any snickering or looks of disapproval would not be tolerated. And there was hardly a man or woman in attendance who didn't already know who Deidra was.

Andre half stood from his seat and raised an arm to invite Edward and Deidra to their table situated in a back corner. Deidra nodded in return and did her best to avoid Nikolas's eyes. She knew he was studying the details of her body language. The grip she had on Edward's arm was affectionate and familiar, leaving him to wonder how close their friendship really was and if Edward was the reason she didn't want to give him a chance to prove himself to her again.

Andre, seated to the left of Nikolas in their darkened corner of the room, leaned in close to his ear. "What's up with that?" He, too, was studying Mr. Bloodgood's close proximity to Deidra.

"What's up with what?" Nikolas replied with a snarl on his face. His eyes were still on them as they stopped to order a few drinks at the bar.

"With Deidra and Bloodgood." Andre knew he was pushing Nik's buttons.

Nikolas began to shake his knee up and down while making a fist with his hand. "I don't know, Dre. Do you know?"

"No, man." Andre smirked and sat back in his seat. "But you'd better watch your ass. Don't let it get in the way of things. We need his help."

"I know."

"You know how much I like the girl, but she isn't worth it."

Nikolas took a deep, controlled breath and exhaled it as he watched Deidra lean over the bar to thank the bartender. Her smile sent a chill to his brain. "Yes she is."

"Eddie," Deidra began in a sweet, calm voice that she topped with a fake smile. "As soon as we get our drinks, we're going to sit with them, find out what it is that he wants, and then get out of here as fast as possible."

"Agreed."

Something didn't feel right to him. As soon as they walked through the door, it seemed as if the looks of disapproval directed at them were not as bad as they could have been. Something about their *lack* of disapproval seemed unsettling.

Her eyes shifted about the room anxiously. "Yeah, I think I'm hungry for some Italian food. Should we stop for take-out on the way back to your house? I mean … I guess I should ask first if it would be okay if I came over." She laughed uneasily.

"What is going on?" Edward asked. He nodded at the bartender as he placed two bottled beers in front of them. Edward put a twenty on the bar top and waved off the change.

"Nothing."

"No, something is definitely going on," Edward replied. They both grabbed their drinks and started to walk to the table Nikolas and his associates were seated at. Edward walked ahead of Deidra, pacing them. He needed enough time to get more information out of her. She was behaving strangely. Even stranger than usual.

"Well," she started slowly. She now worked to counteract his pace, hoping to speed things along. "Um ... I used to hang out here sometimes."

Edward bumped his knee into a chair occupied by a large, bearded man in a leather vest. "Excuse me. I'm sorry."

"No problem, sir," the burly man responded with a polite smile and a nod.

Edward looked back at Deidra as he kept walking. "Oh, so you already know these people? Is that why no one's been trying to kick my corporate ass ... yet?" he joked.

"I don't know. I'm sure they know it's okay for you to be here. I mean, this is Nik's place."

"Nikolas owns this place?"

Deidra smiled. "Not financially."

Edward glanced at Nikolas. He and Andre were watching another man prepare two seats for their arrival. "Why would you hang out in a place like this?" he asked quietly enough not to offend anyone within earshot.

"What's wrong with bikers? Two of my brothers ride and I think they are very misunderstood people. You know, it is very ignorant of you to think that all bikers are hooligans—"

"Deidra, seriously?" Edward stopped in his tracks and turned to her abruptly. "I have criminals and convicts on my payroll! Why would I judge these guys or anyone else at this point?"

"I don't know." She looked at him with guilt hanging in her eyes.

"What's going on with you?" Edward whispered.

She looked over his shoulder, aware that Nikolas and his table of lawless subordinates were watching her and Edward as they stopped only feet away for an awkward, semi-private, last minute exchange. "Nikolas and I dated," she confessed.

"I got that from last night. I'm not *that* dim."

"For two years," she added.

Edward's eyes bulged. "What?!"

"Let's sit down now and get this meeting over with, okay?" she recommended with a smile.

Edward clenched his jaw and turned slowly to face Nikolas. Nikolas stood to greet him and motioned for both Edward and Deidra to take the seats placed in front of him at the round wooden table covered in beer bottles, leather gloves, and cell phones. Two men stood against the wall behind Nikolas and Andre, subservient and loyal.

"Good to see you, Mr. Bloodgood," Nikolas said with a dry, business-like smile. He sat back down into his seat after a quick glance at Deidra.

"Yes, I just asked Deidra how to get here and she seemed to know *exactly* where it was," Edward said with heavy sarcasm. He was doing his best to keep his focus and to let go of things that were beyond his control. A disturbing fake smile cut across his face.

Deidra looked at Nikolas and Andre to gauge their reactions.

"Well," Nikolas's eyes met Deidra's nervously before he turned them back to Edward's. "She's got a good sense of direction."

"I told him about us. I don't care. No one cares. He doesn't care either. Who would? Let's just get this over with, please." She sat in her seat and took a drink from her beer.

Andre snickered.

"Uh ... about what?" Nikolas asked with a faker smile than Edward's.

"You cooking with those ghost peppers again? It doesn't matter. Let's just move on. What's going on? Why are we here?" she asked coolly.

"Um ... okay. I ..." Nikolas shifted uncomfortably in his seat for a moment. "I only asked Mr. Bloodgood to meet with me. I didn't mean to inconvenience you, Ms. Bonaparte. You seem like you are in a hurry for some reason ..."

"Okay then," Deidra stood from her seat. "I'll go. Have a nice talk."

"No!" Edward grabbed her arm. Everyone at their table and the tables surrounding them froze in place. The smile had left him. "Sit, please."

"Let me the fuck go so I can leave. He doesn't want me here, and I don't want to be anywhere near his egotistical machismo act anyway," she stated calmly.

Edward turned to Nikolas and Andre. "I invited her to join me, and this will be the last time any of this unresolved crap will go on between the two of you, got that? I know you were together. Solve it another time or don't solve it at all. For whatever reason in life, we are all here now. So let's work together and play nice." He looked at Deidra. "She's staying. Is that going to be a problem, gentlemen?"

His tone was commanding. So much so that it surprised Deidra. She looked at Nikolas, waiting for his response. Nikolas hadn't expected Edward to be so direct.

He was beginning to think that he had read the guy wrong. Completely wrong.

"Deidra," Nikolas began, in full control of himself. "Please have a seat." He then turned back to Edward. "I am more than happy to have Ms. Bonaparte join us. I respect her research and place great value on her input when it comes to business matters. All I ask is that she have the same respect for me in return ... because ... she's mean."

"And scary," Andre added.

Edward released his hand from Deidra's arm, and she slowly sat back into her seat. She ran her index finger around the rim of her mug while she stared at Nikolas's fingers as they tapped against the table top.

"Okay. I think that's a fair request. Right, Deidra?" Edward asked.

"I'm not mean. And he's lying to you," she replied quietly.

"Excuse me?" Nikolas jumped forward in his seat. His lip curled and there was an angry crease in his brow.

"He has *never* respected my research and he thinks it's a joke. He goes along with things to get paid, that's all." She then looked at Edward. "He doesn't believe in the paranormal. Franklin never exposed him to any of it anyway. The only jobs he gave these guys had to do with collections, and most of them were based out of town—*away* from the races. He's out of his element here. If he goes along with it, he'll be doing it to humor you, just like he did with Franklin."

She then looked at Nikolas almost apologetically before looking down to her lap.

Andre cleared his throat. "I believe in that stuff."

"Is that true?" Edward asked Nikolas, ignoring Andre.

Nikolas gave him a half-shrug. "I do what I'm told and get the job done. What do my beliefs have to do with it?" he asked.

Deidra leaned in. "It matters when we are dealing with this stuff as part of a job. We have no use for someone who thinks of it as a joke. We are talking about huge investments here and something called 'positive particle thought' that you wouldn't care to understand. Your *disbelief* would be getting in our way and endangering our mission. We are talking about huge investments here. We can't fail."

"Okay," Edward placed both of his hands down on the table in front of him and looked at Nikolas. "Why did you want to see me tonight?"

Deidra leaned back and shook her head in disapproval before glancing at Andre.

"What?" Andre asked. "I like ghosts. You don't believe me?"

"How am I scary?" she hissed to Andre.

Edward glared at her before directing his attention back to Nikolas. "Well?"

Nikolas motioned to the other two men standing nearby to step away from the table. He then waited a moment before speaking again. "I talked to Martin. He's willing to come up."

Deidra folded her arms and rolled her eyes. "Great. Did you tell him why we need him?"

Nikolas smirked. "Yes. I described the video to him."

"You don't believe in cases of possession," she said. "So what convinced him to come up? I'm sure you told him it was all bullshit."

"I told him we could hang out and do some riding," Nikolas answered.

"Oh good. Sounds like fun." She turned back to Edward. "You see what I mean? He's not in it for the right reasons."

"I got him to come out here, didn't I?" Nikolas asked sharply.

"We'll see about that." Deidra was fuming at the thought of her own brother jumping at the chance to hang out with Nikolas again.

"Look," Nikolas directed at Edward, "I'll do what I can to help you out. I'm reliable and trustworthy. I can take care of things, no questions asked. I got Martin to come to Dallas. He's coming. I told him why you guys wanted him here, and he agreed to check it out."

Edward nodded. "Thank you."

"Now, if you ever need my help for anything … cover-ups, surveillance, or any evidence you need destroyed … you guys know who to turn to. My guys have worked for the best and are good at what they do. Even *she* can't argue that. No one can touch us. Most of us are, or were, in law enforcement. We have cells all over Texas and some that stretch across the whole country. We even have some cells in Europe. That's why I asked you to meet me here. I wanted to let you know that we can help each other. I'm reasonable, fair, and honest about my services. I would like to work with your organization again. Being connected with you guys opens us up to more jobs that help cleanse society on a much grander scale. You've got a lot of people in high places." Nikolas stopped to take a breath. "That's all I want out of this. Connections."

"How did you lose touch with The Society before?" Edward asked.

Nikolas eyed Andre for a moment while running his hand through his thick hair in contemplation. "Franklin asked me to take care of a guy that we couldn't prove had committed a crime. We don't kill bankers or corporate wastes of space just because some other suit is angry at them. We take care of sinners. The kind that hurt children, women, and men in violent, unthinkable ways. We get rid of *real* evil."

Edward sipped his beer. "So you walked away from the job?"

"I simply told him we didn't have anything on the guy, and I turned him down. He didn't like being turned down." Nikolas then looked over at Deidra to make his point.

Edward squirmed slightly in response and hoped that Deidra wouldn't go into some defensive tirade over the insinuation. "I appreciate the offer. We are currently restructuring some of our payroll, and I will definitely keep your club in mind. What you did for us out at the track was very generous ... and heroic." The seriousness in his voice leaked through into his eyes as he directed the comment toward both of the men seated across from him.

"Thank you," Andre said on both of their behalves.

"We called you here to tell you something else, also." Nikolas took a deep breath and removed his hands from the table. He folded them in front of his chest in mid-air and began to bend his fingers back, popping his knuckles in the process. He then eyed Andre to take over the conversation.

"We want this ... possession issue taken care of as much as you guys do," Andre began in a deep voice that Deidra always thought could have gained him a lucrative side-career in narration. "Two of our guys in the PD are pretty messed up over this. They are on a forced vacation and being put through hours of therapy."

Deidra had to interject. "Experiencing something like that can be severely traumatic. It's more than just the visual part of the experience that's disturbing to witness. When you combine that with the other sensory parts of it—the smells, the unnatural auditory experience, and any kinetic or electrical disturbances that may have occurred—the whole thing can rock your sense of being."

Nikolas raised his eyebrows. "You still in that special doctorate program?"

"Kind of," she answered and looked away in shyness.

"That was good stuff," Nikolas added.

"Shut up, Nik." Deidra rolled her eyes.

"I'm being serious."

Andre looked down to his cell phone. "If Martin can help Vincent, I think it would help the guys to get over it. I don't want them losing their jobs over this. Maybe he could also visit with our two officers?"

"I'm sure he could do that," Deidra said. She turned to Nikolas. "When is Martin getting here?"

Nikolas looked at her. His hardened face immediately softened. "He said some time later this week. He's thinking Friday."

"What's today? Tuesday?" Edward thought aloud.

"Is he staying with you?" Deidra asked Nikolas gently.

"Yeah. But how long do you think this could take? On Monday I have to accompany Congressman Montemayor on a road trip," Nikolas informed them.

Edward perked up. "Congressman Montemayor?"

Nikolas relaxed his shoulders a bit and showed them a half-smile. "He's a family friend. Says he'd feel safer with some security with him on some trip he's taking to a few cities next week. He wants to keep it low-key, so … I guess I'm stuck hangin' out with the guy for a few days."

"If Deidra's brother has to stay past the weekend, my place is always available," Edward offered. He looked to Deidra for some sign of approval with his offer and caught her staring at Nikolas.

"Yeah," she replied in a trance-like voice. "If this is what I think it is, it's going to take more than a weekend to clear it up."

14

When Father Martin pulled the oversized door open, a wave of guilt rushed through his body. It had been months since he had stepped inside the house of his heavenly Father. The time off that he had requested "to think about things" had been granted, and, at the time of the request, an absence from the Church seemed appropriate to him. Almost therapeutic. Martin Consuelo Bonaparte was grasping at any means necessary in an attempt to find the essence of himself again. And he was no good to the Church if he was in fear for his own life.

"Give me strength, Father." Martin stepped onto the carpeted walkway that would lead him between the pews and toward the sanctuary. There was an elderly woman kneeling in prayer in the last row toward the back. Another woman who looked to be in her forties sat to the far left in the middle section of the church. The bluish hue and glossy shine of her chemically blackened hair captured the colors of the stained glass window above her. Her clothing was dark, and on her face was a look of deep sadness. She turned her body and her eyes met with the priest's. There was now a look of expectation on her face.

After glancing around to see if there might be any others visiting the church that he may have missed, he looked toward the altar and lectern, then made his way toward them. With each step, the material of his cassock moved with him in that perfect rhythmic sound against his legs.

He glanced at the statue of Saint Patrick and quickened his pace as he felt that the black-haired woman seated in the middle part of the church was now watching him with great interest. In his peripheral vision, he noticed her posture suddenly straighten. Martin's focus remained clear—this cleansing would be for him ... not them.

When he reached the sanctuary, he was compelled to immediately lower himself to one knee. He bowed his head in respect and then looked up at the tabernacle. Martin took in a deep breath through his nose while, at the same time, closing his eyes. He released it gently and with great concentration.

"Father?" a frail voice whispered from behind his left shoulder.

"What?!" he exclaimed with surprise. "My dear Lord. You frightened me. I'm sorry."

She appeared unfazed by his being startled. "Father, will you be taking confession today?"

Martin looked past her to be sure the older woman in the back had not also followed him up to the front of the church to bother him. He turned his body to face the woman requesting his services and then looked to the ground between them. Avoiding her stare was all he could think of to do at that moment. "I ... I am in a hurry today. I have only stopped here before leaving the city ... to pray for a safe journey."

The woman stood leaning with one hand resting on the pew beside her. She studied the priest's hair momentarily and frowned inquisitively. "Will you be traveling far, Father?"

Martin's eyes darted about the floor. "Yes," he answered and then turned back to face the altar again. He placed his hands together in prayer to prove to the dark-haired woman that he was, in fact, about to be quite busy speaking to God.

"Where will you be going?"

Martin scrunched his face in response to the question and decided not to face her when he answered. "Dallas."

"Then I guess you will be driving since you said it would be far," she replied. "Because it's only about an hour by plane from San Antonio to Dallas."

"Yes, dear." He turned his head halfway to finish speaking to her. "If you would like to have a seat and wait, I will see if I have time to hear your confession when I am through."

The woman smiled joyfully. "Thank you, Father!"

She took a seat on the pew and watched as the blessed Father returned to his prayers in front of her. She wondered how he got his hair so shiny. She then imagined him getting ready in his bathroom with a bottle of hair gel in hand and then pushed the thought out of her head the second she realized that, in that thought, he was shirtless and quite toned. She then worked very hard at trying to stop guessing the name of the cologne he was wearing.

Martin closed his eyes and deepened his thinking into the farthest reaches of his mind. The outside world could not bring him to the resolution he was seeking. He needed to reach within for the question, or questions, to ask before attempting to ask them. He was at an impasse with so many issues in his life.

"Heavenly Father," Martin whispered aloud, "give me the strength to enjoy spending time with my sister on this visit to Dallas. I ask that you guide me in understanding her ways. I know she's not perfect, but she is still my only sister."

Martin glanced briefly over his left shoulder to confirm, to his disappointment, that the woman was listening just behind him, before continuing.

"Heavenly Father, I ask that you protect my sister, her friends, and myself as we embark upon this journey to save one of your children from harm. Though I am unsure that he is in any real danger because ... seriously ... I doubt that Deidra knows what she's talking about in this matter. Anyway, I make this voyage in your name to find out. I pledge to you that I will do my best to serve in your name and to do what I know is right, even if it isn't exactly what the clergy would want of me ..."

Martin glanced over his shoulder again, annoyed. It had been a habit since childhood to pray out loud when he wanted the prayers to count the most, and the overly-needy woman sitting behind him wasn't about to change that. He decided to lower his voice into a much softer whisper now.

"Holy Father, I ask that you guide me to do what is right. Not only with my sister or with my indecision when it comes to the Church, but also with the casting out of any demonic entity that may reside within the man named Vincent that I will soon be visiting."

The woman behind him leaned in closer to get a better earful, not sure that she had heard the priest's words correctly.

Martin continued. "If I decide that the man is indeed possessed, I will purify and prepare myself as best as I can with what I have available to me, and I will confess my sins.

Because ... I have plenty of sins to confess ... but ... that's okay. I will confess them later. You don't need to hear about them now. They aren't that bad ... well ... never mind that part that I just said. I was drunk that night. So ... most of them *are* actually ... quite bad. That's why they are called sins ... I guess."

Martin let out a loud sigh. His eyes welled up and burned painfully. He placed his hands down onto his lap and collapsed back into a sitting position on the carpet, lifting his head upward. "Lord help me fight the demons!" He said loudly into the air above him. He rose to his feet and continued to look upward. "Don't let Deidra get in my way or piss me off in Dallas! She always starts every fight we have and it's not my fault! I do *every ... single ... thing* I can to be patient with her but SHE'S CRAZY! Remember when she was ten and stole all that candy ... and then BLAMED ME?! YOU SAW IT! IT WASN'T ME! How can I cast away evil when she's getting in my way?! How will I focus? She ruins everything, Lord!"

Martin made a fist and pressed his eyelids shut as tight as he could. He did his best to stop the anger he could feel rising from within. He decided to lower his voice back to a safe whisper in an effort to prove that he was still in control of his faculties.

"Forgive me, Lord." Martin looked down at himself in shame and brushed his hands against his hips to wipe away the perspiration inside them. "Just help to keep me from giving in to anger. 'What's up with that hair? Does Jesus know about the designer underwear you have on under that dress?'" he mimicked her voice. "And she's cruel ... 'What kind of a priest rides a Harley? Are you allowed to do that?

You know you just want chicks to look at you. Why don't you just quit already so you can take one home with you?!'"

He paused to catch his breath again. His body heaved like an animal's. "I try not to judge her, Lord, but here I am," he shrugged his shoulders to the heavens, "making an effort to help her with a damned exorcism! The very thing that got me into the mess I am in right now!"

Martin clenched one of his fists and closed his eyes again to help repress the frustration. He forced himself to calm his breathing and to relax his tightened shoulders. "Forgive me."

He crossed himself, unclenched his fist, and opened his eyes. He took in another deep breath and turned in a dramatic whirl to the woman seated behind him and smiled. "You still need my help?"

"No!" she answered shakily. Her eyes were wide and fixated on him. Her upper lip was curled back in terror. She had pushed herself as far back as she could into the pew, hoping the demented man would soon be gone.

Martin happily ignored her reaction to his tantrum-filled prayer and headed for the exit. When he reached the back of the church, he nodded respectfully at the old woman that was still kneeling in front of her pew. She winked at him in return and displayed a toothless smile.

Martin pushed the large wooden doors open with a force that was renewed inside of him and walked up to a silver and black motorcycle parked on the sidewalk next to a bed of crimson roses in full bloom. Its chrome detailing sparkled like fire in the sunlight. He dramatically pulled up one side of his gown to lift his leg over the bike and started the engine. The rumble he felt played for him like rhythmic tribal music and soothed his heart. He put on a pair of black sunglasses and hoped that Dallas would provide for him what San Antonio currently didn't—a direction in which he could be pointed. A purpose ... something ... anything that would be a sign to stay strong and continue to fight through the threats that he had begun to receive again, chastising him for helping those innocents plagued by the relentless demons of hell.

15

Deidra could hear Edward on the phone in his office yelling at someone for something. It didn't really matter what it was that had angered him at that moment. His boss voice was an obvious put-on and it amused her instead of causing her the sense of concern that it should have upon hearing it. In her mind, it was an abuse of authority to fluff up his feathers like that only to spare the person on the other end of the phone a full-on attack. She was very tempted to rush down the hall, take the phone from his hand, and threaten whomever it was with some punishment that would involve a 2x4 with some nails sticking out of it. That would get the job done. She shook her head and sighed at his fluffy mashmallowed version of the corporate anger game.

Line one of Deidra's phone then lit up.

"Yes?"

"There's a gentleman in the lobby that wishes to speak with you," Anthony said delicately enough to cause Deidra to hold her breath for a second in panic.

"Is it the Feds?" She half-stood, grabbing for her handbag, her ear still attached to the receiver as it held her, by a cord, captive to her desk. "If so, all you have to say is, 'We had nothing to do with it' because 'it' covers everything."

"No, Miss," Anthony assured her with a smile in his voice. "It's Mr. Vaughn."

Deidra froze. "Wonderful."

"Would you like me to make up an excuse for you?"

"Uh," she thought on the offer for a moment before answering. "It won't make him go away." She placed her handbag on the desk and listened for Edward's conversation again. When she heard Edward yell into the phone, she finalized her decision. "I'll meet him down there."

When Deidra entered the lobby, the receptionist at the front desk straightened her posture and immediately searched for anything to occupy herself at her desk. The petite blonde tried as hard as she could not to look directly at Ms. Bonaparte as she leaned over her desk, purposely ignoring the man seated on the brown leather couch nearby. He was flipping through a gossip magazine.

"I have a visitor?" Deidra asked the frail-looking receptionist.

"Yes, Miss." The receptionist lifted a finger to point at the man behind Deidra, still working hard not to make any actual eye contact with her. "He's … right behind you."

Deidra turned and glared at Nikolas briefly before taking a few steps closer to look him over disapprovingly. She remembered the times when he would meet her in the lobby, his police uniform always crisp and clean. That now irritated her for some reason. She studied his black chef pants, boots, and the plain black t-shirt he was wearing. He was probably going in to work soon and wanted to stop at Corpotex to cause problems before starting his shift. "Who's chopping up all the onions right now if you aren't there?" she said to him.

"Ha ha. Just thought I'd stop by and subject myself to some mental abuse for a while." Nikolas placed the magazine back onto the oversized table he had taken it from. It definitely wasn't the type of thing that he would normally read, but the bright colors and trashy headline managed to overpower him. "From what I understand, executive chefs usually have other people working on the onions for them."

Deidra crossed her arms and contorted her lips. "Well? What's up?"

Nikolas glanced at the receptionist, suggesting that their conversation wasn't private enough for him and then scratched at his bristled chin. "Can we get some lunch?"

"Sure. Let me call Edward and have him meet us somewhere." She immediately turned to the desk behind her to reach for the phone.

"Wait," he asked. "I meant, just us."

Deidra turned back to face him. She knew how difficult she was being. Of course he wanted to have a private lunch with her, but the feeling wasn't a mutual one. "What for?"

"Because I want to talk to you. We're working together on some things now, and I think it would be healthy for us to," he paused to glance again at the receptionist, "clear some of the tension between us."

"What tension?"

He tilted his head and made a face.

"And since when do you care about the psychological well-being of others?"

Nikolas stood and positioned himself directly in front of her. His blond hair was spiked but messy. He looked down at her face in desperation. "Deidra, please. I'm not good at this," he added softly.

"Fine." She swallowed back the discomfort she was working unsuccessfully to hide from him. "Let me get a few things from my office. I'll be right back."

Deidra tugged at the sleeve of her black polyester blouse as she and Nikolas were seated at the bar. The energetic rush of the Dallas lunch crowd filled the restaurant with animated voices and the clanging of dishes. To her, the bar area seemed to be the appropriate place for them to sit since he was half in uniform and probably in much more of a hurry than she was to be someplace else. Bar service would be quicker. They settled into their tall seats, and the bartender took their drink order—two iced teas, one sweet, one unsweet.

The bar top was a black swirled granite with reflective pieces throughout. It sat atop a mahogany wood detailed with intricately carved rose molding and smooth pilasters.

"It's crowded in here," Nikolas said.

"It's lunch time." She waved at the bartender and quickly pointed at the appetizer she wanted. She didn't need to confer with Nikolas about it because they had shared it in the past.

Nikolas looked at his own reflection in the mirrored area behind crowded bottles of liquor. He then peered upward, noticing the strategically placed lighting illuminating the wine glasses hanging above the blenders and beer taps just to the left of his reflection. "This place is nice. Strange, but nice."

"How is it strange?" Deidra's shoes clicked against the brass foot rail that was fitted along the base of the bar like a shiny snake.

"Well," he pointed at the mirror directly in front of him and waited for the bartender to pass in front of them before continuing. "There's a mirror in front of me. It's distracting."

Deidra laughed sarcastically. "That's only a little narcissistic."

"No, it's just a part of my ... old job." He turned to look her in the face. "I looked in mirrors all day while on patrol. Anything passing in them got my attention, so I'll probably be checking out everything going on behind me the whole time."

"Oh." She smiled. "I think they did that so people could watch themselves get wasted."

"Probably." He smiled in return.

She looked at him and wondered why it felt so natural to push the negative things between them aside for a little while and smile instead. Sitting next to him again had never been on her list of things to repeat in life, but here they both sat. She felt like a traitor to herself. It was difficult not to allow the painful memories to intrude upon the thoughts she had in her head. The organic feeling of his presence sent a panic through her soul. She suspected that his eyes could still suck the tension out of her day in an instant if she looked into them long enough.

"How's work been?" Nikolas asked as their drinks arrived.

"Oh, are we pretending to be regular, upstanding citizens now?"

"Of course." His smile was bright but quickly disappeared again in shyness. "I'm a chef at the most upscale Italian restaurant in Dallas and you ... a corporate go-getter at the most successful software development company in Dallas, right? Nothing but regular people here."

She opened the lunch menu in front of her. "Not really. I *assist* the corporate go-getter. And now that Collin isn't here anymore, I assist Edward."

She hated talking about Collin Bennett. Reliving the ruthless, example-making scare his death was meant to be sickened her. Still feeling the effects his absence left was a torturous nightmare.

"I'm sorry about Collin," Nikolas said with genuine sadness. He knew not to carry on about the topic of his death with her. "Is Edward as easy to deal with … as a boss, I mean?"

"No. Not yet," she confessed. "Collin was a good 'ol boy. He knew the system. Eddie's … new."

"How old is he?"

"Thirty-six."

"A little young to be running a company as important as Corpotex Software, don't you think?"

"I don't know." She looked deep into the menu, hoping to find something light. "He has a lot of help and a great team supporting him. What's the big deal anyway? You're only six or seven years older than him. You are in charge of people."

"True. But I already know that I would run a company of that scale into the ground if I was in charge of it," he replied with a grin.

"Well, that's why you're not in charge of it."

Nikolas ran his index finger across the bar nervously. "Speaking of age," he started. "I wanted to tell you that I have been thinking a lot about priorities and what's important in life."

Deidra nodded before he continued again.

"I know I screwed up really bad before and ... you know. That was a few years ago. I have changed a lot. I haven't even had the chance to tell you the real reason why I left the department and ... I'm different now."

"Nikolas," she said in an appreciative voice. "I know your parents always made you feel bad for not using that culinary degree they sent you to Italy for. You are an artist with food. I just hope you made the career change for yourself and not for them. When it comes to us, I forgive you. If that helps you to deal with working with me again ..."

"That's not what it's about. It's more than that," he insisted.

"Are you afraid I might tell Edward the details of our relationship? Is that what you're worried about?"

"No."

"Then what's going on? You developed a conscience recently?" she asked playfully, taking care not to come across as rude.

"No. It's been there. Trust me. I just ... I have been thinking about where we would be today if we had stayed together. Don't you ever think about that?"

She waited for a few seconds to pass before answering. Just long enough to brace her emotional self for the repercussions of her honesty. "Yes."

Nikolas sighed in relief. "Me too."

"But," she cautioned, "I realize that it probably wouldn't have worked out anyway."

"What? Why?"

"Since you thought I was 'too emotional' and always putting work before—"

"That's not true!" he claimed in his defense. "I mean, I know I said that, but I didn't mean it like that. I'm sorry."

"Look, Nik. I'm going to be thirty-nine soon. No relationship has worked out for me. After you, I was with a psychotic millionaire. Before you, a guy connected with the mafia. I don't have a good record for choosing people. I've given up."

"You can't be serious, Deidra."

"I don't know. Maybe I am." She slumped down in her seat a bit. She was hoping to dodge the subject altogether and nervously rubbed a finger along the shiny silver-colored studs that separated the leather from the wood frame of her bar seat.

Nikolas thought of his approach with caution. One wrong inflection or tone could create a much unwanted avalanche between them. "So this has nothing to do with Edward?"

"What do you mean?" she asked with a hint of defensiveness.

"I mean, he runs a huge company, probably inherited millions, and drives ... what? A black Maserati?" His attempt to seem indifferent about her relationship was failing fast.

"You think I go after money?" Her eyes shot through him.

"No, it's just that you spend a lot of time with him and I just think there's a big difference in being handed everything and waltzing around in tailored suits versus working hard and showing some integrity in life."

"Can we stop talking about Edward? He's where he is in life because that's where he's supposed to be. Everything happens for a reason. Remember?"

Nikolas sighed hard and folded his hands together on top of the bar. His fingers were rough and calloused and the nails on them uneven, chipped in places, and some of them were too short. He slumped his head down in defeat, the straw in his sweet tea almost poking him in the eye.

Deidra couldn't pinpoint why at that moment, but she really wanted to understand his frustration—or at least to be more patient with it. "Can we change the subject?"

"Sure."

"When's my brother supposed to get here?"

"Tonight." In his voice still hung the weight of defeat.

"Today's Friday." She paused. "So we need to try and set something up at the hospital tomorrow morning. Early."

"Not too early," he hoped.

"Don't you two drink too much tonight. This is serious. I talked to Dr. Armstrong this morning. I had to do everything I could to assure him that we were still trying to get in there to help. He said that Vinny made his bed levitate last night. They got it on a cell phone pic. I wanted to shake him through the phone and ask why he didn't take a video of it." She focused in on Nikolas's tattoos. Most of them she was familiar with, but the assortment of culinary knives on his forearm were new to her. "I know you think it will be alright to drink all night with Father Bonaparte because you don't believe in the paranormal, but—"

"Listen," Nikolas turned to lock eyes with her, hoping to convey his loyalty to The Society—and to her. "I *do* believe that something serious is going on. I know that we need to figure it out. I can't control Martin, though. When he gets wasted and starts a few fist fights, I promise to drag him out of the bar and take him home."

Deidra smiled.

"Your brother is like *my* brother."

"Thank you. I'll set everything up for tomorrow. You just be sure to be there when I call you guys. I'm only going to tell you the time ... you know the place already."

"Right. I know. You can text it to me if you need to. My phone is secured."

"You *think* it's secured," she laughed.

"I have connections, too. There's a lot you don't know about me."

"Right. Sorry. I'm used to dealing with ..." she stopped herself before finishing. It sounded too much like an insult when she didn't mean for it to be.

Nikolas did his best to control the smirk creeping across his lips. "Edward?"

Her mouth opened as if to object, but she knew not to. Nikolas Vaughn was a human lie detector. He specialized in the extermination of the country's most vile criminal minds. He was given access to their whereabouts as they awaited trial by attorneys, judges, and officers of the law who were certain that the vicious crimes would go unpunished. And one thing he always made sure to do was to extract a last minute confession before he released them from this world. Deidra never understood how he was able to face those monsters when he was contracted to. It was hard for her to digest.

"Yes. Edward," she admitted. "He's trying, though. Just give him a chance, okay?"

Nikolas nodded at the bartender as he silently delivered their spinach and artichoke dip and placed chips and appetizer plates in front of them.

He looked into her green eyes and remembered the pattern of brown speckled perfectly within them. The detail of her eyes was painfully burned into his memory. He wanted to pretend to wave off any distrust he had in Edward Bloodgood. He also wanted to believe that Edward had the right to be involved with The Secret Afterlife Society.

"This is my favorite appetizer," he said with a timid smile.

Nikolas felt at peace when he arrived for work, entering through the back door of the hectic kitchen. The same could not be said for a panicked sous chef that ran up to him, shoving a menu into Nik's hands. He immediately looked over a section of it and nodded in approval.

"Do you like?" the sous chef asked in a heavy Italian accent. "Tell me now. I will change again for fifteen times if you want."

"*Molto bene*," Nikolas answered. "*Buon lavoro*."

"*Finalmente! Grazie tanto*," the man sighed in relief and turned to a dishwasher standing next to him. "He is *pazzo*, *no? Non lo so* ... crazy!"

Nikolas walked the line, smelling sauces, and reminded the wine steward with a quick wave of his hand that the table red, paired with his newest sauce, needed to be replaced instead with a dryer selection. He then made his way into an office, locked the door behind him, threw his chef coat onto a chair, and unlocked a closet door to step inside it. After scanning his thumb and eye on a hidden security device attached to another door located behind a hanging mess of jackets and kitchen uniform pants, he walked up a flight of stairs. On his way up, he smiled into a series of cameras before stopping at a door to scan himself again.

Inside, three men and two women sat along an array of desks with their eyes glued to multiple computer screens. They were dressed in business attire. Only one man, bringing a coffee mug to his lips, acknowledged Nikolas, but did so without looking away from his laptop or any of the other screens scattered in front of him. "I saw that you didn't bring any food up. Should have denied your entrance." The man then pointed to one of the screens in front of him, divided into four sections of camera angles that faced the stairway outside the door.

"I hate it when you guys work up here," Nikolas smirked. "I can't bring food to people that don't exist."

The agent chuckled in response. "And they say the 'A' stands for agency. And by the way … it's *your* fault we are up here this week. It's not our fault that you happen to be all chummy with Congressman Scumbag. I would much rather be in my own office with real air conditioning and—"

"Thanks. Did you get anything else on Montemayor?" Nikolas asked with authority.

The man with the coffee pointed to the woman seated next to him.

"Yes, sir," she answered. "We found a connection between him and a lawyer's wife named Adrianna Rodriguez."

"An affair?" Nikolas asked with disinterest and some disappointment. It seemed that on every politically connected case his team of agents worked on, affairs popped up. It only complicated things further.

"Possibly, sir. The woman was found dead last week by the San Antonio police."

Nikolas stared down at the paperwork on the woman's desk. "Before or after his bullshit fishing trip?"

"Around the same time, technically. She was found the same morning he was admitted to the hospital in Plano for dehydration."

16

The next morning.

"Slow down. What are you saying?" Deidra searched Dr. Armstrong's words for anything at all, even the most simple of indicators, that might lead her in the right direction. She needed a plan. She could feel the dread in his voice seeping through the phone, reaching her like electricity. Normally she had several different contingency plans for the types of things they dealt with, but this was different. She grasped the phone tighter and her heart was now slamming against her chest uncontrollably. The paranormal was her forte. But in this case of possession—a thing that also tipped into the darker corners of theology—she had no clue in how to handle it. Especially now that something even more unexpected had just occurred.

"They busted through here like a swat team ... all in black. Like in military outfits, but they wore black with black vests. There were machine guns ... it was ... they threw me against the wall. I almost pissed myself."

"Okay, calm down," Deidra advised, hoping for a moment to gather together her mess of rattled thoughts. "So, Vincent's *gone*?"

"Yes!" the doctor yelled.

"That's fucking great."

"No! It's not great!" he argued.

"That was meant as sarcasm."

"I'm sorry!" he panicked into the phone. "What are we going to do? Why would they want him? He was heavily sedated! Once it wears off ... he's going to be levitating things and speaking backward about frosted cupcakes and—"

"What did you just say?"

The doctor sniffled and thought for a moment. "Cupcakes?"

Deidra held her breath and thought about it. "What was he saying about cupcakes?"

"Ms. Bonaparte," the doctor's voice was desperate. She could almost envision him on his knees in anguish as he spoke. "We need to find Vincent before this gets out. I will lose my position at the university, and funding for ..."

"Dr. Armstrong. If I ask you a question, I ask it for a reason. I'm not fucking around here." She had to be commanding. He didn't, and wasn't going to, understand why she was asking, but the topic of cupcakes was important.

"Okay. I'm sorry. I just—"

"What did he say *specifically* about cupcakes?"

The doctor searched his mind before answering hesitantly. "He said ... he wanted me to bring him some cupcakes. I remembered because he had never asked for any other kinds of food. Ever."

"That's all?"

"Vanilla cupcakes," he added.

"Jesus ..."

"With vanilla frosting."

"... Christ."

"He was screaming it over and over. 'Bring me a dozen cupcakes, mother fucker! You better make sure they have extra frosting on them!' It sounds cute but it was horrible." The doctor sighed.

"Alright." Deidra refrained from feeding into the doctor's fears by purposely calculating an air of faked confidence in her voice. "Listen for a moment."

"Okay." His voice shook.

"I will get a team together to look for him. Did you call the police?"

"No! God no!"

"Good," she assured him with relief.

"I thought you guys were kind of like the police. So, I didn't call them."

"We are *better* than the police." She smiled confidently. "And we have more resources available to us. You did the right thing."

She had little time with which to formulate a plan. Candidates for her elite search party were populating into her mind's eye. *I guess I need to get crazy Miguel involved in this.*

"What do I do for now?" Dr. Armstrong asked.

"Just act like nothing's happened. If anyone comes around asking about him who already knows he's been there ... tell them he ... has a contagious disease. Tell them he's under quarantine."

"Yeah ... okay." The plan sounded good to him so far ... sort of.

"I'll let you know as soon as we find him."

And with that unconvincing attempt at having the entire matter under control, Deidra cringed while ending the call on her cell and immediately proceeded to contact Edward.

Five minutes later.

"What?!" Edward yelled into his cell phone, understandably stunned by the news. "Who do you think took him?"

"I have an idea, but I'm going to need your help figuring it out," Deidra explained. "My brother is already here in Dallas. I have to call him and ... delay our original plans a few hours. Maybe."

There was nothing but silence on Edward's end.

"Hello?" she asked.

"Yeah. Did you say a few *hours*? A guy connected to us and our organization is on the loose ... a possessed guy!"

"I'm going to find him," she said. "We need to put together a team to track him down."

"It's 5:46 in the fucking morning! Who are we going to get for this team? It's Saturday!"

"Assassins don't take days off. When I call people, they answer the damn phone, Eddie."

Edward had been in a deep sleep when she called. He realized at that moment that he wasn't yet awake enough to be Mr. Bloodgood the-guy-that-runs-the-secret-society. It was Saturday morning. He was still recovering from being Mr. Bloodgood of Corpotex all week. "Sorry, of course they do. I'm not awake."

"Okay. So, I need you to call a few people that might have been a little too interested in Vinny's condition."

"Like who?" he yawned.

"Government people. I have some names in my head. Anthony knows which ones. I'll have him go to your place and he can go over the list with you. Military connections ... anyone we know that could have found out about Vinny somehow and might have been interested in that kind of ... demonic weirdness."

"Okay. Yeah. But what do I say?"

Deidra's mouth dropped open, stupefied by Edward's lack of distrust in certain facets of the dark worlds they were a part of (and contributing to). The protocol states that the minute something goes wrong, all their enemies, associates, and friends immediately become suspects. He wasn't connecting the dots instinctively yet in the ways that she did. She had to remember that he still needed more time and more training to assimilate properly into her world—*their* world.

"Eddie," she started patiently. "When Anthony goes through the list of groups with you, he will help you to decide who might have Vinny. The questions you ask each group will always be the same. Something like, 'We're missing something important. Do you know about it?' without saying what it is that we're actually missing. Then you end it with, 'Because if you do have anything to do with it, we're going to find out and, when we do, some limbs are going to go missing ... blah, blah, blah, we will crush your skulls ... no ... their balls ... blah, blah, people die.' It's possible that our own crazy fuck Johnny tipped someone off. Who knows?"

"Uh ..." Edward was listening intently. And for some stupid reason, he was now scrambling around for a pen to take notes with.

Deidra thought for a second. "I mean, don't say that to *everyone*. Anthony will help you. You have to be nicer to some groups than others or you won't wake up tomorrow."

Edward placed a hand over his eyes and shook his head. "Deidra, can't we just begin by asking if they know anything about it, then explain that he's a racer and it would be bad to take him since he creates a profit for everyone involved?"

"Tell them he has a contagious disease."

"Deidra ..."

"Okay, fine! Tell them whatever you want! Just give me the info as soon as you get it. I'll get the team together to start talking to Johnny and a few other scumbags we know that might have sold Vinny out."

"Why would anyone be interested in Vinny ... in his condition?"

"Research. The government does their own paranormal research also." Deidra was certain of it. Assisting with government research into the paranormal had been part of her degree plan. "That, or Vinny's in some other kind of trouble. That's probably what it is, you know. He's kind of a d-bag."

"Wonderful," Edward smirked.

"Either way. Get some coffee, have something with lots of sugar in it, and wake up. It's going to be a long day."

17

"I *said* … I'm trying to talk quietly so they don't hear me," Miguel used a harsh whisper as he spoke into his cell phone. He was pacing nervously on the sidewalk outside an office building that had a large sign out front advertising space for rent. His suit was perfectly fitted. He wore a dark purple fedora because he thought that it made him look taller. Not that he wasn't proud to be a little person—he just enjoyed the attention the hat seemed to attract from a variety of women.

"So Johnny was right?" Deidra asked frantically. "They took him there?"

"It looks like it. I don't know for sure. We're still trying to figure it out."

"We who?"

Miguel stopped his pacing to answer her. "Me and Billy."

"I told Billy to stay with Johnny," Deidra said angrily. "Why is he with *you*?"

"We tied Johnny up in his apartment so Billy could come with me." Miguel's voice was calm and collected. To him, tying someone up was pretty routine. Like watering the plants.

Deidra slammed her fist onto the countertop in her kitchen and looked to the ceiling. "Johnny Feinstein is a psychotic, maniac convict. He will probably gnaw through whatever you tied him up with and escape. I *never* told you to tie him up! I need him for stuff! Now he won't ever trust us again!"

"You can't trust him anyway," Miguel tried to explain to her. "Look what he did to Vinny."

"Miguel! I don't know if Johnny had anything to do with this! It's possible that Johnny was *used* by some people so they could find Vinny at that hospital! Did you think about that? Mr. Bloodgood is going to be pissed at you! Have you seen him when he's upset?"

"Eddie? No. I ... I like the guy. He's a ... a good guy," Miguel fumbled his words, trying to imagine Eddie enraged.

Deidra decided to take the opportunity to over-glorify Edward's persona at this point. Not only for the good of The Society's reputation, but as a form of personal entertainment. And she did so while doing her best not to break character and laugh hysterically in the process. "He ... oh man ... he gets all ...like a monster."

"Like a what?"

Deidra's mouth was quivering and her eyes watered. She was doing everything she could to control herself. "When he's mad his face changes and sometimes he drools."

"Oh ..."

"Yeah. And I didn't even know you could use a wine key as a weapon, but he can."

Miguel cleared his throat. "You've seen him use a wine opener thing on a guy?"

"I wish I hadn't, man."

"Geez."

"Yeah. So send Billy back over there to untie Johnny and apologize!"

"Oh man," Miguel said under his breath. "That's why Johnny said that stuff. Maybe some guys *did* trick him into talking."

Deidra wanted to pounce on him through the phone. "That's why he said WHAT?!"

"Johnny said he didn't say anything to anyone about Vinny. He said he only told the cops because they were bothering him."

"What? What are you saying?!"

"Well, after I punched Johnny in the face, he said he swore he told no one about where Vinny was except some cops that pulled him over last night. The cops said they were going to take him in if he didn't talk, and he was worried about makin' you guys mad. You know ... if he went to jail. Now I know why, too. Johnny could've got corked by Mr. Bloodgood."

Deidra blew up into laughter.

"I don't think it's funny."

"No, okay. It's not. Mr. Bloodgood is vicious. Okay, sorry. Is that all he said?"

Miguel worked hard to get past the thought of Edward savagely twisting a wine key into a man's body. Turning and twisting. Piercing ... "Um ... yeah. Johnny said one of the cops grabbed him by the arm and said they were going to take him in if he didn't talk about Vinny and so he told them where Vinny was. He also said ... it's fuckin' strange, but he said he knew where Vinny was because ..." Miguel needed to collect his thoughts before speaking again. He knew that no matter how he phrased the next piece of information, it was still going to sound unbelievable. "He said that Vinny called his cell phone from the mental place a couple of days ago... with his mind."

Deidra was stunned.

"He says it was Vinny beggin' for help. Over and over. Something about, 'Get me out of here. They got me tied to the bed.' And then Johnny asked him where he was and he told him."

"Oh, my God." This was beyond any telekinetic ability she had ever heard of. As insane as it seemed, cases of reported calls from the dead to a loved one seemed more natural to her than this did. Vincent's case was becoming more unpredictable by the day.

"Yeah. I don't get it, but that's what the jerk said. He's a fucking liar. That's why we had to bust him up a bit and then tie him down. I mean, you understand, right? Be sure Mr. Bloodgood knows we didn't mean to upset him, okay?"

She closed her eyes and let the swarm of thoughts continue their endless rotation in her head. She needed to think of a concrete plan to get Vinny back. It was highly likely that his telekinetic abilities were increasing in strength. The phone call—it had to be electromagnetic frequency manipulation. Vincent could have figured out a way to use a nearby cell phone without physically touching it.

"I hog tied him," Miguel boasted for no reason.

"I figured," Deidra replied. "I think Johnny was being followed by G-men dressed like PD. Possibly even Men in Black."

"Creepy freaks," Miguel grumbled. He hated the Men in Black. He had dealt with them before with Deidra, in Del

Rio, and it was an experience he wanted to forget. "Why is this all happening? What's going on with Vinny? Why was he in a mental place?"

"Look, don't worry about that right now." Creases formed on Deidra's face. She concentrated on the way her breathing seemed to be quickening at the thought of Vincent being in the hands of yet another set of people he didn't know or trust. It couldn't be good for his condition. She then wondered what type of research the government might have wanted him for—if it was, in fact, the government at all. It could have been *any* group interested in testing the limits of demonic power. And to Deidra, that was the problem. In the wrong hands, pushing the limits of this energy could not only kill Vincent, but it could unleash something unimaginable and uncontainable.

"Deidra?"

"I ... we just need to get him back. I don't know what's going on. My brother's here. We had to call him. He needs to be with you guys when you go in."

The way her voice trembled alarmed Miguel deeply. She was afraid. "Oh, Jesus. That doesn't sound good. You're starting to freak me out."

"Where's Billy?"

"He's in this building here. We think Vinny's in there. Billy's walking the hallways. Listening."

"You guys are north of downtown?"

"Yes. Before Plano," he answered.

Deidra took in a painful breath and stared into the patterns in the granite counter in front of her. Her plan had to be exact and precise. Each and every movement had to be made with determination and skill. It didn't matter at this point who had taken Vincent because all she cared about now was getting him back safely without losing anyone else in the process. Edward was in enough trouble as it was. They couldn't fail.

Deidra cleared her throat. She didn't know what to prepare Miguel for but felt some need to warn him—to tell him anything that might help to convey the seriousness of it. "I think I know what these people want with Vinny, but I can't let them use him for their own research," she told him. "It's ... not good stuff. You guys just need to stay focused and the recovery needs to go smoothly. No matter what happens."

Miguel understood now that this mission was in recovery mode only. The rules had just changed. This was not any regular collection deal. In a collection, taking the time to intimidate or push people around after you got what you wanted was expected. This mission needed to be clean. "Are we Level Two now?"

"Yes. It needs to be timed."

"I'll let Billy know," Miguel assured her. "He probably knows what room they're in by now."

"Okay. Then get back to me on it right away." The energy was rapidly returning to her voice. "Get back to Johnny after you tell me the exact location. Then return to the building and wait at a safe distance for the next step."

"You got a plan?" Miguel was feeling the contagious excitement in her voice.

"Yeah. I'm going to scare the crap out of these assholes. They have no idea what they just got themselves into."

18

"This is not going to work." Edward was hunched down in the passenger seat of the car, looking upward into the windows of the five-story office building they were parked next to.

Deidra was busy texting on her cell, too busy to look at him. "It will be fine."

Edward straightened himself and turned in his seat to face her. "Whose car is this?"

Deidra smiled and raised her eyebrows. She continued to text feverishly as she shrugged her shoulders. "I don't really know."

"Deidra!"

"You think I'm going to sit around out here in my *own* car? Come on, Boss," she snickered.

"Are you going to return it when we're finished?"

"Maybe."

"Deidra!"

"Of course I am, geez." She looked him over. The intense stiffness in his body looked extremely uncomfortable to her. "Relax. Take a deep breath—"

"How am I supposed to relax?!" he snapped back quickly.

"You want some Chinese food after this for lunch?"

Edward's eyes widened in disbelief. He couldn't wrap his mind around her inability to show some sense of urgency. They were sitting in a stolen car parked outside an office building that was being searched by two hitmen—his hitmen—for signs of a possessed racer that had been abducted from a mental hospital earlier that morning. He looked at Deidra as if her face had suddenly caught fire. He clenched his fists and tightened the muscles in his arms and legs.

"Whoa," she said. "You look freaked out."

"I am!"

"What's wrong with you?" she asked calmly.

"On the phone you said Nik and Martin were going to be here. That means," Edward stopped speaking to count on his fingers, "there's six of us here making a big scene in the middle of the day. How are we going to get Vinny out of there without people noticing?"

Deidra tilted her head sarcastically. "Have you looked around? This is an industrial area. There's hardly anyone here."

"I'm sure there are surveillance cameras!"

"They've been taken care of."

"Where are Nikolas and your brother?"

"They're inside already."

"When are they going to do it? And how are they going to do it?!"

"You need to calm down, Eddie. That's the whole point of having people work for you. You're not supposed to worry about the 'hows' and 'whens' or the 'whys' and the 'who gets killed,'" she explained while eyeing the screen of her cell phone for any updates that she might receive from inside the building.

"What? Okay," Edward began, while shaking his head. "So then after they get Vinny, where are we going to take him?"

"Uh … baktourhaus," she mumbled and cleared her throat. She scrunched up her nose and braced herself for his reaction.

"What did you just say?" he asked sternly.

Deidra, trying as hard as she could not to laugh, looked at Edward and smiled. "I said we're taking him back to your house. Don't be mad."

"Deidra!"

"If we take him back to the hospital they're going to steal him again!" she argued. "What did that one group tell you and Anthony?"

"They said that *if* they had taken Vincent—that was an *if*—it was only because he owed them money and that they were sorry for the misunderstanding and would return him as soon as possible."

"Which is all bullshit," Deidra interrupted. "As soon as they figure out he's all crazy messed up, they will hand him over to some freaky military paranormal research facility to get the money they were going to beat out of Vinny. *Now* Vinny is more valuable, you see?"

Edward blinked his eyes and nodded his head rapidly. "Yes. I see. And you're taking him to my house."

"You live in a fucking mansion. There's plenty of room."

Just then, her phone lit up with a text message that caused her eyes to bug out. "They're about to kick the door in."

On the fourth floor of the office building.

"On three, kick the door open," Nikolas whispered to Martin. He had his gun drawn and in position.

"You're the cop. You should be kicking the door!" Martin protested. He was dressed in his cassock and decorated in purple stole. Deidra had insisted that he "look the part" or he was going to "fuck the whole thing up" if he didn't. Martin looked at his feet. "You have boots on. I'm wearing shoes. Italian leather shoes."

"*Ex*-cop. Deidra says you have to kick the door open or it's not going to look right," Nikolas explained. He looked back and over his shoulder to see if Billy was ready and in position at the end of the hallway. He and Miguel had been assigned to keep watch for any unexpected visitors to the building. Billy, five-foot-five with a muscular build, was an intimidating-looking man. He purposely fashioned his style of clothing around mob movies set in the 1970s. The most intimidating part of his look may have been related to the fact that he didn't seem to know how out of place this made him seem.

"You should kick the door. You have boots on," Martin urged. "I paid a lot for these shoes with some birthday money my dad sent me."

Nikolas was dressed in his usual weekend clothing: a black t-shirt, ripped up jeans, and a pair of leather motorcycle boots. He owned several black t-shirts, most of them a simple variation of the same few themes—bikes, rock music, and pinup girls from the 1950s. All of his jeans were ripped or covered in some form of garage grease. He never cared about what people thought of his style or the condition of his clothing anyway. "Where's your gun?" he asked the priest.

"I don't need it. The Lord is with me."

"Great," Nikolas said. "Move over. I'll kick the door."

"Thanks, Nik. That's very nice of you to—"

"Hurry the fuck up!" Miguel managed to whisper-yell from around the corner of the hallway. If they had been close enough they would have seen the veins popping out from Miguel's neck and forehead.

Martin and Nikolas both turned to look at Miguel just in time to see Billy waving him away to take his place again at the other end of the hall. But since Miguel was amped up on energy drinks and didn't hear any doors being kicked down in the timely manner they were supposed to have been, he'd left his post to run down the hall to remind them to speed things up. That, and Deidra had sent him a text asking if he wanted Chinese food for lunch.

"Hellz yeah I want Chineze food!" Miguel texted back.

Nikolas pulled Martin by the arm and carefully stepped in front of him. "Get ready, Father."

Martin flashed a large smile as Nikolas moved into position in front of the door and kicked it open with a black motorcycle boot that was covered in scuff marks. As the door violently swung open, Nikolas aimed his gun into the room and pointed it with perfect precision at the face of the first man he saw standing in his view. The door slammed into the wall as Father Martin stepped through the door frame.

"Anyone who moves will die," Nikolas stated firmly as Billy ran into the room and slipped in cautiously behind

Martin, taking aim, with a grin on his face, at the other man in the room.

The two men standing in the room were dressed in all black and covered in perspiration. There were four black ski masks on an office desk and four bullet-proof vests stacked on a chair next to it. The two men raised their hands into the air and studied the faces of their intruders with disbelief.

"Where's the other part of your team?" Nikolas asked forcefully.

One of the men nodded his head backward, motioning toward a closed door at the back of the large, open room.

Father Martin stepped further into the room and pulled out a small plastic bottle of holy water he had hidden inside his long black sleeve and gripped it firmly. He stood strong and stared into the eyes of the two men before him as if seeking through them for their souls. With his free hand, he straightened the purple stole hanging from his neck before making the sign of the cross into the air between himself and the terrified strangers before him. He popped open the flip top of the holy water container with his manicured thumbnail and took in a deep breath.

At that moment, the room existed in a silence that could not be described by any of the men within it. It was stale and calm, but it felt unbalanced. Something else existed there that not one of them could have ever wanted to know about or experience firsthand. And the eerie presence of the tall 6 foot 5 inch priest probably didn't help the situation.

"You are in the presence of evil, my sons," the priest bellowed deeply so that his voice echoed against the abandoned room's walls. "The man you hold captive requires the help of Our Lord and so I ask you to release him to us."

The two men standing in the middle of the room with their arms raised into the air looked at each other and then back to the priest with the overwhelming, and surprisingly commanding, presence.

"We ... he's ..." one of them began to shake as he dared to speak.

The priest took another step forward and relaxed his posture. Nikolas also stepped forward, assuring everyone in the room that he was still keeping a steady aim on the man who had just attempted to speak to them.

The priest held out his hand with his palm facing upward. "We understand that Vincent has some value to you and your superiors, but obviously, the conditions of the situation have changed. He's not well and he needs my help."

"Yes. He ... there's ..." the man sputtered in fear. "We had to sedate him."

"Come forward so that I may bless you. I wish to protect you from the demon."

"The ... WHAT?!"

"First," the biker interrupted, "you will call for your men to step out from the back room, unarmed. Or the both of you will die."

"All of you will," Billy added happily.

"My sons," the priest said in a kind voice. "I do not wish to see anyone hurt. We just need Vincent. You cannot hold him like this. The power within him will overpower you, and possibly transfer into your own bodies."

The two men's eyes widened and both of them looked to be on the verge of possibly jumping through the window.

"No tactical training you have ever had will be enough to prepare you for the demon's wrath." The priest's voice was now increasing in volume and thematic presence. "No weapon will protect you from the hellish nightmare that will be unleashed upon you and your unprotected souls. Soon, the demon will overpower the man-made drug you have given to Vincent, as the human part of him is now being slowly consumed by the evil residing within!"

"We'll come out!" a voice yelled from behind the closed door in the back of the room. "We will come out unarmed! You can have Vincent! This is *highly* fucked up!"

"Yeah," the man Billy had his gun pointed at agreed. "We had no idea this guy was so messed up. Our boss just wanted his money back!"

"Step out of the room slowly with your hands where I can see them, and do not fuck around!" Nikolas called out to the men in the back of the room.

The men complied willingly and stepped out of the room to join their accomplices. Billy's gun followed the two men as they exited from the back room until Father Martin asked them all to kindly drop to their knees.

As Nikolas continued to keep a crisp aim on the men, Billy ran around the room to gather up the men's weapons. After collecting them, he placed them into a black plastic bag he had pulled out from the inside pocket of his jacket.

Billy peeked into the back room with caution before making his way inside.

"Is he in there?" Nikolas called to Billy.

"Yeah. He's here. He's alive."

The priest approached the four men, now on their knees and huddled closely together with their hands held above them. He stood over them and bowed his head. "Let us pray."

19

"Your brother is a badass!" Miguel exclaimed as he and Billy shoved Vincent into the back of the car Deidra and Edward had been waiting in.

"Oh, okay. What did he do?" Deidra asked.

He scared those guys with some evil, creepy church-talking stuff!" Billy replied.

After carrying Vincent down multiple flights of stairs, Billy was out of breath. As soon as Miguel opened the car door for him, Billy flopped Vincent into the back like a rag doll, head first.

Edward apprehensively turned in his seat to look at Vincent. He then watched with his mouth open as Miguel did his best to fold Vincent's legs into the car comfortably enough for them to properly shut the door. "Why are you guys putting him in here?"

Miguel and Billy froze.

Billy leaned in over Miguel to answer. "Deidra said to put him in here after we got him out."

"Oh, good," Edward replied with a soured sort of smile.

"Isn't my brother riding back there with him?" Deidra asked before a finger tapping on her window startled her, causing her to draw in a quick breath. She lowered the window and Martin leaned in.

"He should be all right until we get back to Edward's place. He's been drugged," Martin informed her. "But we've got to get out of here now. Nik is coming down any second. We'll meet you there."

"Okay," she replied with concern.

"Pop the trunk. We took their guns!" Billy announced proudly.

"Put them in your own damn car!" she tilted toward the open back door to reply.

Miguel slammed the back door shut and patted on the side of the car. Within seconds, Nikolas and Martin were on their bikes. They were all now heading toward Edward's place. The deep rumble of motorcycle engines permeated everything around them.

Their caravan of ruffians was headed back into the posh suburbs of the northern Plano area. They had accomplished their mission. Vincent was safe. Anthony and two nurses were waiting for them at the house, ready for Vincent's arrival. This meant that they might have to prepare for a long night ahead. This also meant that, according to Deidra, there were now nine orders of Chinese food to fulfill on the way to Edward's. Deidra didn't forget to promise that there'd be hell to pay if her sweet and sour chicken order was botched.

"He looks so normal," Anthony said to Deidra. He then turned to point to an arm chair and nodded at the woman standing behind him.

"After they take his vitals, I want to get Martin in here to do his evaluation," Deidra responded. She and Anthony stood over Vincent. He laid peacefully in the bed that had been prepared for him only an hour earlier. When Anthony had received the call, he quickly began making the necessary preparations. The two nurses he'd contacted were already on The Society's payroll and knew to arrive in a timely manner. They had been instructed to dress discretely and were asked what Chinese dish they preferred.

Anthony turned to the male and female nurses. They were both dressed in jeans and looked like they could have been a couple when they arrived at Edward's. He waited for them to situate themselves into the chairs he had set next to Vincent's bedside before providing them with instructions. "When you have your equipment ready, you may proceed."

They both nodded in return as Anthony and Deidra exited the room and quietly closed the door behind them. Outside the door, Edward and Martin greeted them with wide-eyed stares and wordless faces of concern. Although there were a few chairs scattered along the dark hallway leading up to Vincent's room, the two of them stood, waiting in anticipation for news of what was coming next. The darkened hallway only added to the sullen mood felt between them. It was decorated with marble statues and paintings that were set into gold-colored frames. From the corners of the eye, the statues seemed to come to life, their shadows crawling on the walls and the floor beneath where they stood. During the wait, Martin had to force himself to cease his anxiety-filled pacing, and the echoes of whispers became intrusive to his thoughts as he second-guessed his presence in Dallas.

Edward hated every part of it. To him, it was an invasion. Anthony had worked to calm Edward's rattled nerves as best as he could. But Edward still reminded Anthony that the guest rooms were designated for guests, and not, as Edward kept repeating, for some paranormal side-show case study.

"He's having his vitals checked," Anthony told Martin in a quieted voice. "They will let us know when he is ready for your evaluation. They will be helping to wake him up in a bit. Would you prefer that they vacate the room while you ...?"

"Yes," Martin answered solemnly.

"Not a problem, Father."

Edward and Deidra waited for the results of Martin's evaluation while eating Chinese food out of polystyrene containers in the kitchen. When Deidra thought she heard the faint sound of a door opening and closing echo through the hall, she dropped her fork into her rice and jogged toward the sound. Edward grabbed a paper towel to wipe his mouth before following.

As she and Edward approached them, Martin and Anthony appeared to be in an intense conversation. Martin towered over Anthony like a giant. His ominous black attire only added to the seriousness of their situation. They both turned to look at Deidra as she approached.

"Well?" she asked as patiently as she could.

Martin's eyes scanned Anthony's and then Edward's face before he returned his attention back to his sister. "He's not possessed."

Deidra was in disbelief.

"Sorry," Martin shrugged.

"No ... that's good. I mean, he ... but ... maybe the drugs haven't worn off enough yet," she said quickly. "We have a video and—"

"I understand," Martin said softly. "But he's just not showing the signs. I promise you ... I looked him over carefully. I wouldn't just tell you something like that without truly believing it."

Deidra looked away from him, knowing how sensitive he was to her mannerisms. She didn't want him to pick up on any misdirected disappointment she might express. The disappointment she felt was certainly not due to any question about his expertise. Instead, she feared the unknown force that now occupied Vincent's mind.

"What do you think it is?" Edward asked.

"Well," Martin began. "Usually it turns out to be a mental disorder of some kind. Some psychokinesis maybe. The movement of objects with the mind has been linked to possible schizophrenia and other disorders, but it's more visible in teens than in a man of his age."

"He was in a car accident," Deidra added. She seemed to be coming to some sort of a realization about Vincent's condition.

"He still has some bruising on his head. It looks like he was in a pretty bad one," Anthony said.

"There have been cases of psychokinesis that started after a head injury," Deidra continued, with a dazed look in her eyes. "It doesn't explain the changes in his face or voice when it's happening. Or the coldness in the air around him, though."

Martin tilted his head and frowned. "I'm sorry, Deidra. I wish I could help, but this one's out of my hands."

"But the doctor couldn't find anything either," she reminded him.

"I'm sorry," he repeated again, understanding her frustration.

Edward cleared his throat as quietly as he could, hoping to remind them of his role in the now increasingly complicated situation. "Um ... so what are we supposed to do with him now?"

"That's the problem," Deidra pulled on the onyx and silver pendant hanging from her necklace while mentally debating what steps to take next. Once she had seen the video in Edward's office of Vincent growling and scratching at the bed sheets, she was convinced that he was possessed. An exorcism was the only thing she had considered as a solution. There was no backup plan. "I guess I can call Dr. Armstrong again. I'll see what he recommends after I give him the news."

Edward scratched his head uncomfortably. "But he's not staying *here*, right?"

"Let me call him and ... I don't know what to do," she answered.

Martin patted Anthony on the arm and then held his hand out for Edward to shake. "I'm Martin."

"Yes, sorry," Edward jumped to attention and grasped Martin's outstretched hand. "What a way to meet, right? I'm Edward."

Martin chuckled. "I agree. Still, better than never meeting at all."

"Yeah."

"Well, Deidra," Martin said as he looked himself over to check that his cassock was still neat and in place. "This has been quite a morning ... no ... afternoon. But, I need to get changed and meet Nik for a few drinks. I think he left already. I'm probably leaving tomorrow morning since he has to travel out of town tomorrow night or the next morning or whatever. Is there still some Chinese food?"

"Yeah ... uh, okay," Deidra mumbled. She felt displaced. Dismissed. Part of her, even though she was preoccupied with the inconvenience of Vincent's unknown condition, wanted to shake her brother and ask him why he wasn't interested in spending some time with his only sister instead of a drinking buddy he only thought he knew. "Great. Have fun."

Martin smiled at Edward while attempting to do his best to ignore the panicked look on his face. "Okay. So ... nice house, Ed." He then made his exit alone by walking down the long hallway, leaving them standing in a huddle of mental confusion.

Something sounded like it slammed against the door behind them inside Vincent's room and broke into a million pieces.

"Wonderful," Edward said.

20

Monday morning.

Edward was swamped at work. The morning began with a teleconference call during which a client was somehow dropped from the line midway through the meeting. He was then interviewed by an ambitious university student for a campus newspaper feature on young professionals before rushing off to meet with his senior staff over doughnuts and coffee. But he found it hard to concentrate on the topic being discussed as the floaty things in his coffee were a bigger distraction to him than they should have been.

To complicate his morning further, Anthony was being forced to assist him from home. Edward's home. There seemed to be no end to Vincent's unexpected stay in the now seriously trashed guestroom. Even though it had only been two nights, Vincent's unearthly screams and contorted eye-rolling had caused the departure of one of the two nurses and kept Edward up throughout the night. After Deidra convinced Dr. Armstrong to visit early Sunday morning, the continuous and moderate sedation of Vincent helped make it easier to endure.

Edward was startled awake from a daze when his cell phone rang. "Yeah," he answered.

"Where are you?" Deidra asked in that paranoid-fueled voice that Edward loathed at this point. And at this point, it was only Monday.

"In my office. Please tell me everything is fine. *Please*," Edward emphasized with desperation in his voice.

"Did you eat breakfast?"

"I had some doughnut-type of thing. It had jelly in it." Edward made a face. "I don't even know if it could be classified as a doughnut but it was round. I got some of the jelly on my hands and now my keyboard is all sticky."

"You sound grumpy."

"Well, I haven't slept much in the past few days." His voice was a cross between hostile and mad—British mad. Not American mad. The high-pitched tone of his voice indicated further that he seemed to be on his way out mentally. "There's a strange guy at my house that *I did not invite*. He scares me. I think I'm going to have to check into a hotel."

"Why don't you stay in the pool house?"

"Why the fuck should I stay in the pool house at my own home?! Why isn't *he* in the pool house?!" Edward's words blasted intensely through the phone.

Deidra could almost feel the pain that must have been throbbing in Edward's temples. "He needs to be in the house where he can be checked on," she reminded him. Edward needed to be consoled, but there just wasn't enough time. "Look, that's not what I called about. Sorry about your stupid doughnut and Vinny."

Edward took in a shaky breath. He closed his eyes and braced himself by tensing up his face muscles. "Just tell me what blew up. I'm ready for it. Go ahead. I'm fine."

"Okay …" Deidra dismissed the dramatics. "I just got a call from Nik."

"Oh, that's nice. Did he ask you to lunch again?"

Deidra felt her breathing halt for a few seconds. "How did you know about that?"

"What does it matter?!" Edward asked with a rabid look across his face. "You are free to do what you want. I just think that a guy that ditched you years ago isn't worth shit. That's all. Do I respect his contract work? Yes. Do I care who he is otherwise? No. Am I stalking you around town to see who you have lunch with when it isn't with me? Occasionally. But only because I care."

Silence.

"But please do continue," Edward insisted harshly. "So he called you becaussssse …"

"What is wrong with you?"

Edward sat forward in his seat and placed his elbows on the desk. "If you want me to be that damn pushover you knew before all of this," he paused to draw a frantic swirling pattern in the air above his desk with his finger, "… it's too late. That Edward is dead." Edward swallowed hard and now wished that he had ingested the coffee that was over-populated with mysterious floaties. Maybe then he would be able to think clearly. "If you want an *actual* friend that will tell you how it is, then that's me."

Deidra couldn't believe what she was hearing.

"He's a joke."

"Edward!"

"He's insecure and has some hero complex, which, by the way, I'm sure you are impressed with."

"Eddie, I'm not … this isn't what I called about! And *by the way* … that lunch was to discuss getting past our issues so we could work more effectively with you!"

"I have to go," Edward said. "My face is twitching and I need to clean my fucking keyboard! Too many 'w's are coming out at once when I type and it's all like, 'WWWWWWRFTWWWWW!'"

He then ended the call without feeling an ounce of guilt.

21

They had all crammed into a large, black Chevy Tahoe. Their road trip had begun at about 7:13 a.m. in front of the congressman's office in Dallas. They had each shoved a piece of overnight luggage or a duffle bag into the back and settled in for the ride. Their first stop would be in Austin.

The plan seemed simple enough. Congressman Montemayor was set to make short public appearances in four cities: Austin, San Antonio, Uvalde, and Del Rio. They planned to spend the night in a hotel in Del Rio. The next day, Tuesday, he was scheduled to attend a luncheon hosted by the Del Rio Chamber of Commerce. Then they would all head back to Dallas with only one stop in San Antonio for a dinner event Tuesday night for the sheriff's department. The congressman hoped that they might find the time to visit the border town of Eagle Pass after leaving Del Rio on Tuesday afternoon, but their driver didn't like the math. Their time would be limited, and there were four people the driver was shuffling around—the congressman, his security guy, the assistant, and himself.

They were an hour past their stop in Austin when the congressman started mentioning that he wanted to stop there again on the way back. Austin had been quick. An hour after having breakfast downtown, they were meeting and greeting with the people at 9 a.m., just as planned. The news reporters asked minimal questions, and the photographers snapped a few photos for some small section in the paper. Montemayor walked a few halls of The University of Texas and purchased a shirt at one of the campus bookstores, shaking as many young voters' hands as he could along the way. He turned to his assistant once to remind him that he thought it was amazing how kids came from all over the place to study at that campus. The assistant knew what he meant—the hand-shaking was like an investment into the future. Noted.

They arrived in San Antonio around 1:30 p.m. and took time to stroll along the much celebrated River Walk. Unfortunately, it was similar to torture for the congressman's entourage since they had missed lunch. So when Nikolas hovered over an outdoor menu along the way, the assistant Phillip took notice and reminded Mr. Montemayor of the time.

"Well, of course!" he answered in a chipper tone. "Let's get some lunch. Mexican? Come on, boys! San Antonio has the best Mexican food!"

By 5 p.m. the sights and sounds of historical downtown San Antonio would be miles at a distance behind them as they took the Loop 410 west to Highway 90. They were now headed towards Uvalde, their last stop before hitting the border town of Del Rio, Texas.

And it was at that point, while on the 90, headed in the direction of Mexico, that the quiet ex-police officer, Nikolas, started to notice something strange going on. Fernando Montemayor was twitching. It was faint and hardly notice-able at first, but Nikolas could actually feel it happening because they were seated together in the back. Each time the congressman flinched, Nikolas would pretend not to notice as he looked him over and waited for the next one to occur.

After about five minutes of this observation, the congressman suddenly jolted upright.

"Pull over!" the congressman said with a start as he cupped his mouth with both hands.

"He's going to be sick," Nikolas told the driver.

"All right ... hang on," the driver cautioned them as he switched into the slow lane and then carefully maneuvered them onto the narrow shoulder.

"Here!" the assistant turned from his spot in the front passenger seat and handed back a plastic convenience store bag. "I have a few more of these up here if you need them."

Nikolas took the bag and opened it for the congressman and then held it steady under his chin for him.

"Thanks, Nik," Fernando whispered. He took in some slow, more controlled breaths as the SUV came to a complete stop on the side of the highway.

"We'll be in Castroville soon," the driver tried to assure them. "Maybe he needs some medication. His doctor can call something in to a pharmacy. Maybe some of that motion sickness stuff."

"Yes, thank you, Smith." Phillip jumped out of the vehicle and rushed to open the congressman's door for him. "Here, sir. Fresh air. That's what you need. Some air."

The assistant then looked inquisitively at Nikolas as he scooted across the back seat and closer to the opened door. The illness seemed almost sudden enough for it to have been food poisoning, but Phillip now wondered why it wasn't affecting him or the security guy. Phillip had ordered the same plate as the congressman—chicken enchiladas. "How's your stomach? Do you think it was the food?" the assistant asked Nikolas.

"I'm fine," Nikolas answered. He now sat on the edge of the seat and leaned out, hanging an arm on the side of the door, watching the congressman. "You?"

"Oh, yes. I'm fine, also," Phillip answered back with a polite smile.

Congressman Montemayor then looked at Nikolas, rolled his eyes back into his head, and convulsed violently before falling limp into the grass.

22

5:47 p.m.

"We should be in Uvalde by seven," their driver said to them without daring to take his eyes off the road.

"I'm fine," Fernando said to Phillip, waving his hand dismissively into the air. The assistant was turned around in his seat, staring back at him with concern. "Turn back around. Put your damn seatbelt on. That's all I need ... to be pulled over and you've got no seatbelt on. Christ almighty ..." his words trailed off into mumbles.

"You gave us a scare, sir," Nikolas said in Phillip's defense.

The congressman looked embarrassed and turned to peer out through his window. He wished that the night would arrive quicker so they could ride in darkness. It would feel more covert to him. Less exposed. And he hadn't looked forward to the coming of night for a while. This time, he had people around him. The fear wasn't as strong. He knew that somehow this entire thing had something to do with—

"Are you sure you're feeling okay?" Nikolas asked.

"Yeah. Come on. It was the heat. God damn ... that heat hit me so hard when I stepped out there ..." The congressman's eyes shifted back and forth. "If you guys had called an ambulance ... how embarrassing. I fainted. That's all."

Aliens. They did something to me on that lake. I know it.

The congressman scratched at his chin and then coughed.

Nikolas looked him over, unsure of what to think. Vincent's face flashed through his mind for an instant. Something about the twitching leading up to the fainting spell stuck with him. "Will you be up to eating? We're meeting with the mayor at a steakhouse right off the highway. Should be in an hour."

"Of course. I'm fine." The congressman smiled. "Just let me take a nap. I'm tired. That's all."

"Okay. Good idea."

7:12 p.m.

Their arrival in Uvalde was quiet. Nikolas stared out the window, taking in the small-townness of it all and Phillip flipped through emails on his phone as the congressman snorted in his sleep.

"We need to wake him. He'll probably need a coffee," Phillip suggested to Nikolas.

Nikolas tapped Fernando gently on the arm. "Sir, we're in Uvalde. Did you want us to stop for coffee before we get to the steakhouse?"

The congressman groaned. "No. I'm good. Thanks."

Nikolas was concerned. Not so much for the congressman's health but more for what may be affecting it. Chef

Vaughn was pretty sure that Fernando—a warm, light-hearted family friend—may be down-playing a medical condition, even a psychological one, perhaps, that he did not want preventing him from pursuing his political aspirations. But *Agent* Vaughn was almost certain that it was guilt seeping through Fernando's consciousness. That guilt was branding him like cattle. Something in his nervousness spoke volumes. It hung in the congressman's eyes with extreme weight.

To Nikolas's disappointment, there had not been one moment during the trip so far that left him alone with his suspect. Nikolas was only able to observe up to this point and was careful to keep a safe, trustworthy distance. Fernando had hardly spoken a personable word to him anyway. It was odd. The man was practically his uncle but was being unusually cold. Preoccupied and distracted. There was a great deal on Fernando's mind and Nikolas—Agent Vaughn—was determined to figure it out. Not only because he had been assigned to but also because of a dark, gnawing feeling building up inside him. There was something very different about this case. Something he couldn't put his finger on.

"I could really use a steak," Fernando said to Nikolas. "You still hunt out this way with your uncle?"

Nikolas smiled. "It's been a while."

"He invited me. Almost every time he went hunting, I got the invite. But you know what I did? I turned him down. I wish I could … go back and say yes." The congressman sighed reflectively. "When we get back home, I'm going to call him and set something up. Life is too short."

"I agree."

"We can't live with regrets."

They pulled into the restaurant parking lot. Phillip grumbled about his legs being asleep and then checked his emails again while he walked in ahead of them to check on their table. The driver offered to wait in the car, but the congressman refused to let him. He invited Smith to join them for dinner.

Nikolas followed a few steps behind the rest, taking his time to straighten his suit jacket and to shake out a cramp in his leg. He glanced at his phone as he stepped out of the Tahoe and then watched as the congressman paused ahead of him to scratch at his neck. He was scratching so intensely that it pained Nikolas to watch him do it. Then the twitch returned a few times, jolting through Fernando's body like a current of electricity. A few careful steps closer to the restaurant entrance, and then it was gone.

Self-conscious, Fernando immediately looked back at Nikolas, wondering if he had picked up on the unsettling behavior. Their eyes met for only a second. It was clear to him that Nikolas had seen, and was doing his best to avoid reacting with anything but a concerned smile.

23

"What kind of a play was that?" Edward asked Deidra. She threw her cards down onto the dining room table in a lighthearted sort of huff and looked around anxiously. A spark appeared in her eyes as she thought of something.

"Oh no." Edward knew that look. Deidra was cooking up an idea.

"What?" she asked.

"Tell me what you're thinking."

"This poker game sucks. I'm going to check on Vincent."

Edward twisted his lips and recoiled. "Why? There's a nurse in there. He's fine."

"I want to ask him some questions."

"Oh. So, that's the idea you had. I knew I saw something going on in your eyes," Edward said with a smirk. "What kind of questions?"

Deidra placed her index finger down on a red gummy bear that had been sacrificed to become part of their ante. She pushed on its squishy belly while pondering the right words to use. "I've been thinking about a few things Dr. Armstrong said Friday morning when he called to tell me that Vincent had been taken."

"Like what?"

"Well … like something about cupcakes." She looked at him intensely, hoping to see it connect with him.

"What did he say about them?" Edward was now very worried about the implications. The frosted treats gave him nightmares. Not too long ago, he had witnessed an alien tongue licking at a cupcake through the plastic mouth of a human mask during a meeting. The little tongue lapped at the frosting at such great speed that all he could see was a blur around the mouth area of the mask while the grey alien watched his reaction through its fake human eyes. He was certain that one of the only reasons they attended meetings was for the promised cupcakes. He just didn't see why else they would even care to pay attention to the primitive ramblings of humans.

"Vincent wanted vanilla cupcakes."

Edward tapped his fingers on the table. "Let's find out what he was talking about."

Vincent's eyes were glazed over, just as they had been for days. He stared at the ceiling, his face expressionless. Edward and Deidra asked the nurse to wait outside the door. Then they sat in two armchairs placed close to Vincent's bed. Edward motioned for Deidra to begin her interrogation.

"Hey, Vinny," she began softly.

No reaction.

"Um … okay. Listen, Vinny," she tried. "I know this whole thing has been … crazy? I guess that's not the right word to use. Better than the word 'insane,' but still not good. Maybe … interesting. Yes, interesting. It's been very interesting." She looked over to Edward and shrugged.

Edward made a rolling motion with his hand, encouraging her to continue.

"We're still trying to figure out what's going on with your ... situation. I hope you understand. We really are trying," Deidra went on to say.

Vincent still stared blankly at the ceiling. His mouth was parted slightly and the only movement from his body came from his chest as he took in and released weak, shallow breaths.

Edward decided to speak his part. "Sorry the priest thing didn't work out, Vinny."

"Yeah. That was Mr. Bloodgood's fault."

Edward glared at her.

"Okay, but seriously ... you need to start eating again soon. This whole IV thing can't go on forever. The doctor from the hospital told me that you would like to eat some cupcakes."

Vincent's eyes suddenly blinked. He turned his head to the right to face her.

Deidra sat up straight in excitement. "Is that right? If so, I'll go right now and get you some. Chocolate, right?"

"NO!" Vincent growled. "Vanilla."

"All right. Good." She flashed a quick glance at Edward. "I will get some for you."

"Now?" Vincent asked, lifting his head from the mattress. His eyes were filled with excitement, but the surreal deepness of his voice reminded Deidra to be cautious.

"Yes. Right away. But first, I need you to tell me one more thing."

Edward braced himself for her next question to Vincent. He hadn't ever seen Vincent communicate this calmly. He seemed more lucid now. Perhaps Dr. Armstrong had changed his dosage of medications. Maybe he had switched him to something new.

"What do you want from me, Deidra?" Vincent whispered. His eyes were bloodshot and the wrinkles collected around them were very recent.

She pitied his new, haggard-looking face. "What happened to you before the car accident?"

Vincent groaned. "There is no '*before*.'"

"Vinny? Did you do something before the accident that you shouldn't have? Did you meet with investors without telling us?"

Edward scooted to the edge of his seat.

Vincent put on a crooked grin. "He doesn't belong to you. He's ours." His voice sunk into a deeper grumble.

"*Ours* who?" she pressed.

"Give me a fucking cupcake." Two horrible voices at once.

"Vincent," she leaned in closer to him, "did you defect?"

Holy shit! Edward understood everything all at once. *He's racing for the greys?!*

Vincent's eyes fluttered. "Money is money is money is money is money is money is money is—"

"Vincent!" Deidra stopped him. "What did they do to you?!"

Vincent's eyes jittered harder until there was nothing to see in them but the whites. "Humans need chemical adjustments before they can race on other worlds. Your races are boring. We are bored … your parties suck."

"Oh my God," Edward breathed out.

The air around them grew cold.

"Vincent, what did they do to you? Did they inject you with something? Is it an implant?" Deidra's voice was in a frenzy. She knew she was getting closer.

Vincent smiled. It was an awful, wicked smile. "I know something you don't know," he sang like a child.

Deidra tilted her head, confused. She was ready to play the game. "Then tell me."

"Give me a cupcake. I will tell you."

The lights in the room flickered and a light bulb popped, causing her and Edward to jump.

"I will," she promised. "I have to get them from the store first. Just tell me now. Tell me what you know because I'm starting to think that you don't really know anything. You're lying."

Vincent scowled and flicked his wrists under the leather straps. "Your politician is tainted," he replied.

"What? That doesn't mean anything to me. Who?"

"Montemayor deserves worse than what he was given. To burn in hell would be paradise ... to burn on Earth is more fun for everyone. Lessons to be learned ... and now everyone in his path will learn it ... and fear it. They are in danger. They are in danger because he has angered the Great Seeker. Hell's fire is upon him. Hell's fire. Burning. Itching." Vincent laughed like a hyena until he went into hideous convulsions.

Edward shot up and ran to get the nurse as Deidra ran for her cell phone.

24

After Nikolas read the text message on his phone he replied, "I can't talk, but I can text. Are u ok?"

The reply from Deidra came in quickly. "Yes. Are u next to Montemayor?"

"We are sitting together in Tahoe on way to Del Rio."

"WTF? U didn't tell me u were going there!"

Nikolas turned toward his window for some privacy. "I didn't want to upset you."

He then waited anxiously for her reply while focusing on the fields of overgrown grass, mixed in with the cactus, rushing past his window. Even in the dark, he could see that their scenery had changed from lush green fields to patchy desert. The sun had set in the direction they had been driving in, causing several complaints from Smith and Phillip. Now, in the silence, he remembered Deidra's mother.

"Ok," she texted back moments later. "Vinny is talking more. He said weird stuff about Montemayor."

"Like what?" Nikolas typed into his phone.

"Is Montemayor acting strange?"

Nikolas pursed his lips together just slightly before responding. "Yes."

"Kind of like Vinny is acting?"

"No, but odd physical behavior. Some memory loss. At dinner he forgot a lot of past events." Nikolas looked around nonchalantly and faked a yawn.

The driver took notice. "We should be close to Brackettville soon. That's about 20 minutes from Del Rio. You know, my mom lives in Del Rio. I got an aunt in Brackettville. I know this area pretty well."

"Yeah, that's good news. Can't wait to get into a bed. You plan on seeing your mom while we're there?" Nikolas said to Smith.

"I'm going to stay with her tonight." Smith smiled.

Nikolas looked at the congressman. "This drive is killing my back. How are you doing over there, sir?"

The congressman groaned and turned to his window. "I think that steak wasn't cooked right. I'm not feeling very good." He worked his fingers along the controls on the door, reaching for the right one to open the window.

"Shit. We need to pull over again," Nikolas called out to Smith.

"Yes, sir."

Another text came in from Deidra. "I REALLY need to talk to you!"

Nikolas only had time to glance briefly at the text before the congressman clutched Nikolas's arm and scanned his face with wild panic in his eyes.

Nikolas flinched in reaction. "Sir?"

Phillip was already out of his seatbelt, looking back at them, his mouth gaping open without words to speak.

Smith had pulled them over to the shoulder of Highway 90. "It's pitch black out here. This part of the highway is dangerous. Be careful."

The congressman opened his mouth to speak as his hand gripped even tighter onto Nikolas's arm, but only a hoarse breath escaped him. The driver turned back to let them know that they could go ahead and get out if they needed to, but froze at the sight of the congressman's frenzied face, and gasped.

"Sir?" Nikolas asked. A simple blip sound indicated that his phone was continuing to receive texts. "Let's get outside for a minute and get some air."

The congressman nodded in agreement, then closed his mouth. His facial features were stiff and ridged as if paralyzed. In those widened eyes, they could see that he was frightened of something. "Air," he said as his breathing quickened. "Air."

Nikolas kept his eyes on the congressman. "Phillip, get out and open his door."

They all knew that this was more than food poisoning, and it definitely wasn't car sickness. Phillip pulled the back door open and waited in silence.

"You can back out now, Fernando," Nikolas instructed.

The congressman nodded blankly and Phillip reached in to help guide him out. Once they were standing, Nikolas looked him over. Fernando was drenched in a heavy sweat.

"Let go of my arm so I can help loosen your tie," Nikolas said in a firm voice. "You don't look well."

"Nik?" Fernando loosened his claw-like grip and began to tremble. "Something is wrong with me."

"I know."

"I'm awake, but I see a nightmare in my head." Tears then began to fall from the congressman's face. He took an uneven step backward.

"What do you mean?" Nikolas asked. "Phillip, get a water."

As Phillip ran to the opened passenger side door to grab a bottled water, the congressman fell to his knees in the dirt. He looked up at Nikolas. Pain smothered his face. "I did something bad in San Antonio." He wept and pointed a finger to the sky above. "Then they came. They did something to me."

Nikolas was stunned. "What did they do?"

"I don't know! They got me out on Lake Hubbard! They almost killed me."

Phillip kept his distance behind Nikolas as he watched his boss sobbing on the ground.

"You didn't bring me along with you because of some threatening emails, did you?" Nikolas asked him.

"No. I was abducted. The nightmares … I see death. I smell blood," he sobbed harder.

Then Nikolas and Phillip watched as the congressman fell onto his back and into fits of convulsions.

"Do we hold him down?" Phillip yelled.

"No! Stay back," Nikolas commanded.

The congressman's jaw appeared to be ripping itself apart from the inside. The mandible scraped from side to side, the angle pieces protruding sharply against the jawline of the skin. The crackling and tearing sounds weakened Phillip's stomach, and he turned away to vomit in the grass.

"What's happening to him?!" Phillip screamed as he wiped his mouth with the back of his hand.

"Get inside!" Nikolas yelled. He pulled out his weapon, aimed it at the congressman, and took a step back. The convulsions had stopped. The congressman was now clutching his abdomen and folding himself into a fetal position. He rocked back and forth in agony. The seams of his shirt started to pull apart and stretch. The congressman's body appeared to be growing.

"Fernando!" Nikolas yelled.

Phillip slammed his door closed behind him and watched as his boss then flipped over, landing on all fours. Fernando's features were contorted. He was suddenly unrecognizable as he looked directly into the eyes of the man standing before him holding a gun. The man had his aim on a face that he did not recognize—grossly deformed and covered in patches of thick hair. Fernando was now staring into the man's eyes with a sharp-toothed snarl and an elongated snout. He was no longer human. The animal Fernando had become then crouched back on its hind legs.

"Oh my God! No!" Phillip crumpled his body down into his seat as far as he could and then peeked out to see if Nikolas was going to shoot the beast in front of him. Instead, the monster disappeared, running in a blur ahead of them along the highway toward the next town.

25

"... So, I'm just saying that I don't remember drinking the *whole* bottle. That's all," Martin explained to Malcolm. "I should have left to head back to San Antonio yesterday afternoon, but ... here I am. Thought I'd say goodbye to Deidra and check on that kid again before I go."

Malcolm looked him over and fidgeted nervously. "Uh ... they're running around here somewhere. Mr. Bloodgood said he'd be down in a minute."

"And Deidra?" Martin could tell that Edward's security guy was hiding something.

"Oh ... uh ... yeah." Malcolm looked toward the kitchen. He was overly distracted. "She was packing up some food or something. I'll go look and see. Uh ... can you just ... wait here a minute?"

Martin nodded. Something wasn't right. He watched from the foyer as Malcolm hurried away in a jog and into another part of the house, while texting on his cell. Martin waited patiently for a few minutes until he found himself staring into a small, tinted dome-shaped bubble attached to the ceiling. He hoped that he looked good in his jeans. Then he sucked in his stomach and stood a little taller—just in case he was being watched through the security camera.

Deidra ran into the room, the heels of her shoes clicking into relentless echoes around them. She stopped suddenly before him and worked to catch her breath. "Jesus. You … wear … a lot … of cologne."

"Funny."

"Have you heard from Nik?"

"I talked to him," Martin had to think for a moment as he tipped his head back, "Sunday night. Yesterday."

"Call him."

"Right now?"

"Yes!" she turned to run back in the direction she had just come from. "Call him over and over until he picks up!" she yelled as she left.

Martin pulled out the cell phone from his back pocket.

"Where's your priest costume?!" she yelled back to him from some unseen place.

"It's not a costume!" he yelled in return as he called Nikolas.

"Come over here!" she insisted.

Martin followed the sound of her voice as she continued to speak to someone. The way her words bounced along the walls made it difficult for him to pinpoint her exact location. He could hear her shoes against the marble tiled floor as she rushed around. *This place is a maze.* He heard his call to Nikolas go to voicemail. He passed through the grandest kitchen he had ever seen and then saw a light coming from another room as he turned the corner. It was the room Vincent had been staying in. Now, as a guest in Edward's home, without the stress of facing possible demonic adversaries, Martin noticed its fine details. The intricacies of the crown molding leapt out at him. Deidra's taste in art hung all over the walls. As he walked into the guest room where they'd placed Vincent, the rich reds of foreign rugs stuck out. When visiting as a potential exorcist, none of this had mattered before. "Deidra?"

"Yeah. I'm in here. Come in." She was deeper inside the room in a large closet.

Martin entered the room to see Vincent sitting upright in an armchair. His head was flopped forward and his eyes were droopy. A nurse was removing his IV and there was a straitjacket laid out on the freshly made bed, along with a few plastic freezer bags. Deidra had exited the closet and was now mumbling to herself. She sat down on the edge of the bed and held out her hand, counting something. Martin then noticed that they were syringes.

"What's going on?" Martin asked reluctantly.

She looked up at him and then reached behind her for an over-sized, black leather handbag sitting on the bed and pulled it closer. "Did you call Nik?"

"It went to voicemail. What's going on, Sissy?"

She stopped in the middle of her frantic counting of drug inventory and looked up at her brother. *He hasn't called me that in years.* "We're heading for Del Rio."

Martin was shocked. "Del Rio?"

"We have to. Something's happening. Nik could be in danger," she explained.

"Why?"

"Because! You were right. Vincent isn't possessed, but ... well ... no. He *is* possessed, but it's not a demon. It's an alien. A grey. I think. I don't know what they did to him but I think they did something to that senator Nik is with, also. I don't get it. I mean, Montemayor is connected with The Society, but why any of this is happening makes no sense. Vincent is a racer. I understand why they want him ... but the senator?"

"Congressman."

Deidra put her head into her hands and slumped down. Her elbows went into the handbag on her lap and her breathing became heavy. Martin hurried over to her.

"It's okay," he said softly as he touched her shoulder and sat next to her on the bed.

"No. I ... we have a race in two weeks. They fucked up one of our racers ... they caused all these problems for us and ... I don't understand why! What's the point of all of this?" She couldn't look up at him. "Now some congressman guy, too?"

"I'm sorry."

"We do what our investors tell us to do to keep these people entertained and happy. We created this impossible racing world for them. I mean, it's just something used to impress the aliens while they visit. Something that they actually enjoy about the human culture. And they profit from it! We all do! So we follow their rules and their inter-planetary standards. Why? So the greys can screw it all up behind our backs? So they can throw a wrench in it for fun? Because they're bored? That's why they caused that helicopter crash ... well, I can't prove that, but ... it was probably them! We're running around here like this ... not ever knowing whose side we are on!" She slammed her fist onto the bed next to her. "I don't know how much more I can take from these ... societies. There's no rules. They say there are ... but no one follows them because they all lie to each other and hide their true motives behind every single thing they do. It's like all of the governments ...

ours … theirs … are just killing and pranking each other over and over. And we—the organizers—are stuck in the middle."

"Why did the greys mess with Vincent?" He wanted to calm her down, but also wanted the whole story. "Did Vincent tell you?"

"Yes. In a way. They did it to help him assimilate into racing on …" she looked at him, "another planet. I know it sounds crazy, but it's true. They've been going behind our backs to steal human racers, and … they stole the DNA of classic movie actors to race them against each other before. The Earth investors confronted them about it … it was awful. It's wrong. That's *our* history. I don't understand their obsession with human culture."

"But I thought the races were government operated."

"Well … your government is in a partnership with the greys. They have been for years. I don't know the total extent of the military part of it and I don't want to. All we do is take care of the entertainment part. Whatever keeps them happy—weird parties, cupcakes, and races. And they just love watching us kill each other over the outcome of a race. Like a giant philosophy lesson. And the gambling … what they do with the profit … it scares me to think about it."

Martin pulled his eyes away from hers. Her world was a struggle of convoluted unknowns.

"Martin, I need your help. There are things I don't understand. They scare me. Sometimes, this whole thing *still* scares me. I don't sleep well," she added. "There *is* a place in all of this for faith and spirituality. I know that. Without it, I have no idea how I could keep going."

"Yes. Faith is important. It bonds all of us together."

"Just because I research the spirit world, study the paranormal, and get bossed around by aliens and secret government people, it doesn't mean I dismiss what you stand for."

"But you don't believe, really. Do you?" he asked.

"Martin, please … don't ask me that. Let's not get into this right now," she begged. "I am … Nik is in trouble and … I…"

"Okay. It's all right. Finish getting ready."

She looked him over as he stood. "Where's your priest … cassock thingy?"

"It's in my bag. On my Harley."

"Okay, good. You're coming with us."

"What? Deidra, I have Mass to attend to on—"

"It's for Nik."

Martin thought about it for only a second. He owed Nik for helping with his mother. In his eyes, Nik deserved a sainthood. "Okay. Of course. But why do I need the cassock?"

Deidra nodded toward Vincent and smiled. "Just in case."

"But …"

"Vincent believes that he needs you. The alien part of him doesn't. Vincent's faith might be enough to fight through it. After we find Nik and figure out what's going on, maybe you can … try to help him again. It kind of *is* a form of possession. Besides, you look super cool in that dress. It might help us through some barriers in Del Rio."

"So you're bringing Vincent?"

"We have to. The alien part of him knows something, and we can't just leave him here."

Martin walked over to Vincent and knelt down in front of him. He placed his hand under Vincent's chin and smiled sadly. "Vincent?"

Vincent's eyes—his true eyes—looked at him, unfocused and childlike. "Yes, Father?"

His voice was nothing but a weakened whisper, but Martin was relieved that it was, indeed, a human voice coming through to him.

"I'm still praying for you, Vincent."

Vincent's eyes welled up with tears and his lips trembled. And in a tiny voice, he mumbled so softly that it was barely audible. "I believe, Father. I believe."

26

Nikolas pulled himself together as best as he possibly could. The way the creature had pushed past him in the darkness kept replaying in his head. When it ran, it got so close to him that he could feel the rush of air the thing was able to generate with its intense speed and massive size.

Its face was burned into Nikolas's memory. The light emitting from the back door of the rented SUV had been enough to illuminate the features of the contorted face staring into his own. The primal sounds of panting were terrible. And the fangs ...

"You want me to drive ..." Smith paused to clear his throat after taking in a breath too quickly, "... *toward* it?!"

"Yes. Now!" Nikolas demanded.

"No fucking way!" the driver declared sternly, his teeth chattering.

Nikolas pushed his gun onto the back of the driver's head. "Then give me the keys and get the fuck out."

Phillip's body stiffened against the back of his seat. He half-turned his head to face the driver. "Just do what he says!"

"Okay!" Smith shook as he grabbed the wheel and started the engine. "Can we talk about this first?"

Nikolas's phone rang. "No. We don't have time for talking. I'm a special agent. If you don't drive this vehicle right this minute, I am taking it from you. If you don't want to go along with what I am saying, you can get out right now."

"We're in the middle of nowhere!"

"That won't matter because I'm going to shoot you as soon as you step out."

"Okay! I'll drive!" Smith yelled back. He steered the vehicle back onto the highway and continued driving west as instructed.

Nikolas's phone rang again. "What?" he answered calmly.

"Deidra asked me to call you every five seconds." It was Edward. "Is everything okay?"

Nikolas glanced at the horrified looks on the faces of the two men seated in front of him. "Not really."

Edward pulled his cell phone away from his ear to yell back, "Yes, I'm talking to him!"

"Mr. Bloodgood?"

"Yes?" Edward returned.

"There's a problem here."

"Deidra and I are on a jet waiting to take off for Del Rio. Martin is with us ... oh, and Vincent. I don't know why she wants to bring him, but you weren't answering the phone and he was saying something about that congressman you're with—"

"What did Vincent say?" Nikolas interrupted.

"Um ... something about hell on Earth?" Edward answered.

"Really?"

"Yes."

"That's interesting. You said Martin is with you?"

"Yes."

"I might need him. Deidra will know why. Montemayor turned into a seven-foot werewolf a few minutes ago. How long will it take you to get to Del Rio?"

Edward tried to hear in his head, again, the words he had just heard Nikolas say. "I'm sorry. What did you say?" The pilot was now starting the engines of the luxury jet.

"How long will it take you to get here, Mr. Bloodgood?"

"An hour and a half? I think."

"Call me as soon as you land. Get Deidra to call in a favor at the Air Force base there. The base is called Laughlin." Nikolas then promptly ended the call.

"What did he say?" Deidra asked from the edge of her seat. She had changed into jeans and an edgy black t-shirt for the ride. Her arms, sleeved in colorful tattoos, never seemed to stay still long enough for Edward to admire. She was moving too fast—crossing and uncrossing her arms repeatedly. Edward wondered if Martin's priestly attire was making her feel self-conscious, like the artistically crafted ink on her skin was somehow sinful.

Before entering the plane she was able to get in some last minute complaining about it not being boot season yet and opted for a pair of patent leather flats. When Edward reminded her that she had been wearing boots to work in recent weeks, she glared at him for a second and tried to explain that Dallas was different from Del Rio, but he didn't get it. *There's a different dress code for each city?* he had wondered as she lectured him.

Edward looked at her with a dazed expression. Absurd fashion rules were now the furthest thing from his mind. Nearby, Martin placed a blanket over Vincent and settled into his seat.

"Well?" she prodded.

"Um …" Edward contemplated on the words he might use. "Nik said … Okay, I don't know what he meant to say, but what he did say was that …"

The plane started moving.

"Eddie. Tell me what he said." Deidra's voice was filled with impatience and stress. She was tapping her fingers on her knees.

Martin focused on Edward's face in anticipation.

Edward knew how stupid he was about to sound but decided to say it anyway. "He said Montemayor is a huge werewolf."

Deidra didn't move at all and there was no reaction from her brother. They both looked at him with uncertainty, almost as if he hadn't spoken a single word to them. The look on Deidra's face was the very one that Edward had classified as the 'what-a-freakin'-moron-you-are' look.

"Did you hear what I just said?" Edward asked.

"You guys have some interesting friends," Martin responded. "I should move to Dallas."

"Deidra," Edward said. "Is that a code word for anything? He also said to call the Air Force. He said you would know what that means."

"Know what *what* means?" she questioned.

"Know what *that* means."

Her face soured as she looked at him. "It probably means he's a damn werewolf."

"Well, what are we supposed to do now?! What is going on here?" Edward's voice rose in volume over the sound of the plane gaining speed on the runway.

"Well, I don't know what he's talking about. Either he thinks this congressman *is* a werewolf, or the congressman is suffering from some disorder in which he now *believes* he is a werewolf. Either way, Martin can fix it."

Martin leaned back in his seat, surprised. "What do you mean?"

"I'm pretty sure that one of the werewolf cures is a good old-fashioned exorcism," she told him.

"You think that's the cure for everything, don't you?" Martin asked her flippantly.

"So what if I do? I know my paranormal and occult history quite well!"

"Can you two stop fighting for a minute and explain to me what's going on?" Edward gasped. "Werewolves? Now it's werewolves? Deidra, please tell me that you know how to handle this."

"I don't."

"You've never dealt with werewolves before?"

"Are you serious? No. Of course not. That's insane," she answered. "Do you hear what you're asking me?"

"Then how are we going to take care of this?!"

"Calm down. We're going to talk to your pilot and have him take us to the Air Force base there in Del Rio," she began. "Then, we're going to meet up with Nik and figure out the story, have Martin wave his magical hands over the werewolf guy, and go from there."

"They're just going to let us land at an Air Force base?" Edward asked.

"Yeah. I know some people. I'm going to use some code for … secret stuff."

"Okay. That sounds legit," Edward lied.

Martin let out an exaggerated, attention-getting breath. "I've never done a werewolf exorcism," he confessed over the loud engines. "Werewolves don't exist, soooo … you know. It would be hard to know how to do one. Because of that. You know."

"Really?" Deidra asked, holding back a burst of laughter. "Thanks for letting me in on that. That's awesome."

"Well then, tell me how to do it," Martin challenged her.

"Use that book you have in your bag!" Deidra yelled as the noise inside the plane increased.

"There's no werewolf chapter in it!"

Edward looked them both over before clearing his throat. "Isn't he supposed to ask permission from a bishop or something before doing stuff like this? I saw that in a movie."

Martin put on a large smile.

"Don't worry," Deidra answered him with an all-knowing grin. "He gets his permission from the same people that will help us land this plane on government property. Our society, theirs, and others, are all connected. If there's a werewolf, he'll be allowed to take care of it."

"The world isn't exactly the way they tell people it is," Martin explained to Edward. "You'll get used to it soon enough."

27

The man in the black suit approached the man from the sheriff's department with urgency in his stride. The deputy was standing outside a white SUV that was detailed in orange and black. He stood with his arms crossed and his brow furrowed, glancing back inside at another deputy in the front passenger seat. When they received the call to meet with the man in the suit, it sounded government from the start. Government, and untrustworthy.

The two deputies had been told only three things—the man's name was Nikolas, his vehicle was a black Tahoe, and the vehicle's location would be outside the front gate of the Air Force base and across the highway, behind an old building. And when one of the deputies asked for the reason behind the secretive meet up, he was simply instructed to take whatever action the man told them to, and to do it discreetly.

"Good evening, sir," the deputy said to the man in the suit. He left the door open behind him so that the other deputy could listen in on the conversation. "Juan. Nice to meet you, Mr. …?"

"Nikolas."

The deputy looked down momentarily to the man's dress shoes and then slowly moved his eyes back up to assess the details of his black suit before figuring out what to say next. Looking over Nikolas's shoulder, he counted two other people seated inside the large, black Tahoe. "How can we help you tonight, Nikolas?"

The man in the dark suit studied Juan's nametag and then his face. The man's expression was as blank as the deputy had expected it to be. "What were you told about the situation so far?"

"Just to meet up with you here. I'm still not sure why, though," the deputy said. He was careful not to look at the man standing across from him with any readable emotion in his eyes. He wasn't comfortable with the fear he'd heard in his superior's voice earlier on the phone. There was definitely something different going on. He could feel it.

"Juan," Nikolas began to explain. "I hate to do this to you guys, but I have a job for you that you may not enjoy too much."

"That so?"

"Yes, sir." Nikolas looked at his cell phone to check the time. "In about 20 minutes … maybe more … a private plane will be landing at that base across the street there. I'm pretty sure the Air Force will be making themselves available to escort the passengers of that jet to my location—wherever that may be at the time of their landing. If not, you will be escorting them."

The deputy looked him over again. "You're not going to wait for them here?"

"No, sir. You're going to stay here to keep a watch on my friends in the Tahoe until some people from inside that base are ready to care for them."

"Excuse me, sir," the deputy spoke as kindly as his ego would allow him to at that moment. "You want me to watch your friends here until some Air Force people come and get them?"

"They've been through a lot and may need medical attention. An Air Force doctor is going to evaluate them to make sure they're all right. Until then, they need to stay here while I go where I need to go. And I don't want them talking to anyone about anything. You understand?"

"Yes, sir."

"When the doctor is available and ready, he or she will have someone from their security personnel meet you here to escort them inside the base. At that time, you will either be released or asked to escort my friends from the jet to my location," Nikolas instructed.

"Yes, sir."

"That's it," the man in the suit said.

"We wait here and watch over these guys," the deputy pointed at the Tahoe, "until a plane lands and some military police come to let us know what to do next."

"Yes."

The deputy ducked his head a little and looked back at his soon-to-be babysitting partner and raised his eyebrows. When he turned back to Nikolas, he only smiled awkwardly.

"I do have a quick question for you, though, Juan."

The deputy's smile disappeared. "Yes, sir?"

"You got any unusual radio activity this evening?" Nikolas wondered.

"No, sir," Juan answered. "By unusual, what do you mean?"

"Well ... large dog attacks, bears ... anything that seems like it doesn't fit."

"We've had bears here before, but not today." The deputy smiled dismissively.

Nikolas's eyes lit up. "You've had bears out here before?"

"Yes, sir. Driven our way 'cause of some fires."

"I see." Nikolas contemplated the information. "Good to know. Hand me that radio of yours, please. I'll get it back to you."

The deputy's shoulders tightened immediately. His mouth became visually tense. Reluctantly, he reached for the radio attached to his utility belt and then unclipped the mic attached to his shoulder. He surrendered it, with a look of uncertainty on his face, to the blond man with the hardened features standing before him.

Nikolas then turned to make his way towards his vehicle and proceeded to open the front passenger-side door. After a few brief words, the two men inside got out and walked over to the deputy. The deputy looked the men over and could see that one of them was trembling and showing signs of what he recognized to be shock.

The man named Nikolas then got into the driver's seat of the Tahoe and quickly left them.

Juan knew by the looks on the men's faces that something felt terribly wrong. "You two all right?"

No answer.

"Why don't you both have a seat in the back," Juan suggested. "It's too humid out."

Silently, they both complied. The three of them took their places inside the Sheriff department's SUV and sat in uncomfortable staleness for almost a full minute before a radio crackled to life.

"Available units in the Del Rio area … there is a disturbance at Greenwood Park. Reports of an … unknown … large animal. We are receiving multiple calls. PD and Game are responding but may need possible backup."

"What in the hell?" Juan whispered out loud.

"It's *him*," Phillip trembled harder now than before. There was a darkened pitch to his voice and it shook as he spoke.

"Who?" Juan's partner asked as he turned eagerly to face him.

Phillip's eyes stared in hardened fear at the deputy looking back at him. "I'm not supposed to say." His words stumbled out of him feebly. He looked much like a child awoken from the crest of an appalling nightmare.

The radio then came alive with activity, with voices scrambling over one another in desperation to be heard.

"Can you copy that?"

"It ran through the middle of the street!"

"… yes, sir. Garfield Street?"

"Yes!"

"PD is calling for EMS. It slammed right into people!"

"We have deputies on scene … if I tell you guys what they told me …"

"… over seven feet tall!"

"… all fours, man! Running on all fours!"

"I saw its face!"

"What did it look like?"

"I saw it, too. It's fast."

"Jesus, man. It's a ... it has fangs!"

"This isn't our thing. Someone needs to call in some ... government people on this."

"Does anyone have a location on—"

Juan held his breath as the radio went silent.

28

When Edward's jet landed, several high-ranking military officers were there to greet them. The Base Commander assured them that any assistance needed would be provided at a moment's notice. An offer of vehicles was made which included select military drivers, and Deidra nudged Edward to accept them even though he had already planned to do just that. He wished that she would notice how fast he was catching on.

"We'll only need two," Edward stated. For whatever they were about to face, Edward took it upon himself to place Vincent and Martin into a separate vehicle from his and Deidra's. Deidra had convinced Martin to change into "a real priest" before leaving Edward's house. She explained how important it would be to psychologically impress the authorities. It was a lesson of many she had given, and would continue to give in the future, pertaining to the art of human engineering.

"Your friend there," the commander pointed toward Vincent as he spoke, "doesn't look too good. We can care for him medically until the situation is contained, if you would prefer."

Vincent had succumbed to some twitching and eye fluttering again as his dosage of morphine started to wear off. Deidra had placed him into the straitjacket, but left it unfastened and hanging loosely on him due to the humidity outside. He was muttering things under his breath. Things about frosted cupcakes and how he couldn't understand why people were not working harder to provide them to him.

Edward nodded in appreciation as their group was hastily escorted on foot across the runway to their SUVs. "Thank you, sir. If it were up to me, I'd take you up on that offer. Unfortunately, we need him to come along with us."

"Understood, Mr. Bloodgood."

After a quick phone call to Nikolas, it seemed to take them only eight minutes to make it to the historical section of downtown Del Rio. And after the short crossing of a bridge that led them over a railroad track, they were right in the center of the chaos that had overtaken a celebration in the small grassy area the city referred to as Greenwood Park.

Deidra gasped at the circus-like spectacle before them as their vehicles squeezed through the crowds of people gathered on the streets and on the grass. "There are too many people here. They should have been cleared out."

"How do you get them to leave?" Edward asked.

"You get all of these cops to pack up and go. That's how." She answered while waving a finger around.

"Do you see Nik anywhere?"

She looked down to her cell phone. "I'm texting him."

Their driver stopped in the middle of the road with the other military vehicle following close behind. Curious citizens were blocking their way.

"Can't go any further, sir," the driver informed them. "We are jammed in."

"Nik's up ahead talking to some police officers," Deidra said to Edward. She put her hand on the back of the driver's seat. "We'll get out from here. Let your guy behind us know that we'll be right back. I want his passengers to stay inside."

"Yes, ma'am."

Edward and Deidra proceeded to exit their vehicle and did their best to maneuver through the crowds of bystanders and witnesses while taking in bits and pieces of conversations along the way. Deidra walked on her toes just long enough to peer over the shoulders of those blocking her view. She spotted Nikolas up ahead with three police officers, all of them huddled together in deep conversation next to a local PD squad car.

As they approached, Edward and Deidra waved at him. Nikolas only glanced at them for a moment and then frantically waved them over.

"This is quite a big scene," Deidra said to Nikolas.

"Tell them what you told me … about the incident. Start to finish," Nikolas said to one of the officers standing next to him. His tone wasn't so much authoritative as it was eager. His suit jacket had been tossed aside someplace unseen and his sleeves were rolled up. The black shoulder holster he was wearing stuck out against his white shirt. Perspiration drenched his face, neck, and chest. "Quickly."

"Nik. We have to get these people out of here," Deidra reminded him.

"I know, but you need to hear this first."

All of them focused on an officer in his early thirties. He wiped his brow and adjusted his posture into a more professional-looking stance. On his face hung the weight of the story he was about to tell.

"I responded to some calls that came in to dispatch about fifteen minutes ago," the officer began. "When I arrived on scene, some kids were crying and about twenty adults ran up to my car at once. They all started describing some … creature that ran through the park while the kids were performing. They were dancing and playing music. Something for their school, I think. It knocked over some of the children. I called for EMS, you know … because they were all shaken up and—"

"Tell them how the creature was described to you," Nikolas said. His voice was hurried.

The officer's face then changed. He looked at Edward and Deidra and gave them a smile filled with what appeared to be embarrassment. "I'm not saying that what they think they saw was … real, but—"

"It's all right. Just tell them."

"They told me that it was very large. Like a man, but more like … a wolf. Its fur was dark gray and some said more brown or tan colored. It was running like a dog, but … faster. If they are describing it correctly, on all fours, it would have been as tall as I am." The officer glanced into the faces of the two other officers standing beside Nikolas. He sought their approval, but they each looked away in shame. They both knew that they could corroborate their stories alongside his, but hoped that they wouldn't be asked to say a single word on the topic. At least, not on record.

Edward stepped in closer. "Did any of your officers see it?"

The officer hesitated. "I don't know." His teeth chattered.

"Which way did it go?" Edward asked.

"It took off down Garfield." The officer turned to point behind him and beyond the dozens of witnesses and spectators who seemed to be increasing in numbers.

"Where does that lead to?" Deidra asked.

"Mexico," one of the other officers interjected.

The third officer standing next to Nikolas turned up his radio and waved his arm for their attention. "Listen!"

"*... through the back yard and then broke through a fence. Ramirez reported spotting it in the Terrace area and Customs informed us that it approached the port and made a sharp right at great speed, possibly heading for the airport area or near the fence.*"

"It's closer to the border," the officer explained.

"They're talking about the *border fence*?" Deidra asked.

"Yes, ma'am."

Nikolas tapped on the screen of his phone and then took a step backward. "We need to clear out this area. Get all of your officers out of here. Tell all of these people to leave. They need to get inside their homes. Immediately."

"Yes, sir."

Deidra stepped in closer to Nikolas and frowned apprehensively. "Why are they taking commands from you? Who are you calling?"

Nikolas held up a finger and placed his phone to his ear and listened for a second to be sure that his call was connecting. Seconds later, he turned to her with a smile that was created more with his eyes than with his mouth. Rolled up a quarter of the way, his sleeves hung loose so that his sporadically placed tattoos peeked out just enough to prove that he might have a personality hidden behind his stern demeanor. She pushed away a warm memory of him jokingly comparing himself to David Beckham as he poured her a glass of wine to accompany her perfectly prepared chicken marsala.

"Maybe they like my tie?" he answered with a dry wit.

She smirked, not buying the act at all. "Who are you calling?"

His face grew serious. "Homeland Security."

29

"We've found two here in the brush ready for trans-port," U.S. Border Patrol Agent Ruiz said into his radio.

"*10-4. I'm en route to your location.*"

He and Agent Cooper had pursued the two illegals from on top of their horses for over three hours, with a canine agent in the lead. Upon catching them, the canine agent and his dog tracked down the bundles of drugs hidden several feet away in the brush.

Agent Ruiz got down from his horse to get closer to one of the men they had just captured. The man sounded like he was wheezing. "*Esta bien?*" Ruiz asked with concern.

"*Si.*"

"You don't look good. *Ambulancia?*" Ruiz bent down to get a better look at the two men sitting in the dirt.

"No. Tired ... and hungry." The man's English was broken.

"We'll get you some food and water soon. *Comida y agua.* Okay?" Ruiz said to him as he patted the man once on the back. He stood as he saw the canine agent approaching and heard the sound of a truck arriving in the distance.

"There's just the three bundles of dope. There was probably another guy with them," the canine agent suggested. His German Shepard winced and pulled on her leash.

"She alerting on something?" Ruiz asked.

The agent looked around in the darkness. "I don't know. She's acting strange. I think there's another scent in the air."

A green and white truck pulled up and parked a few feet away. Another agent got out and greeted them with a smile. "Good catch, Talamantez," he said to the canine agent.

"She did all the work," he responded, nodding toward the dog.

"We've got some guys on a possible third from the group, but he's probably headed for the river by now," the agent from the truck said. "Hey, Cooper? We still watching the fight at your place?"

"Yeah, Juarez," Cooper replied. He was still on his horse, waiting for the right time to get the animal back to the trailer.

"You guys hear that stuff on the radio about some bear?" Juarez then asked.

Talamantez threw his head back in laughter. "Yeah, I heard it."

Ruiz shook his head in comical disbelief. "I ain't got no time for some damn bear. What are we supposed to do with that shit? Fuckin' bears would scare the hell out of my horse. Those damn game wardens should be out here taking care of it."

Without warning, Cooper's horse lifted its head into the air and let out a forceful snort. Its body tightened and its ears perked upward. "Jesus!"

Ruiz's horse immediately followed suit, bringing its legs in closer together and shifting on its hooves back and forth, anxiously stepping in place. Then both horses showed signs of wanting to pull away. Something out toward a patchy group of trees was frightening them.

"Shhhh," Ruiz said to his horse while gripping the reins in his hand.

Agent Talamantez stepped away from the horse patrol agents with caution as his dog crouched down and pulled on its leash, urging her handler to move them away from where they stood.

"What's going on?" Agent Juarez asked in a hushed voice. "Do they hear something?"

The men they had captured earlier scooted in closer toward the agents. After reading the body language of the animals, they were eager to get away from the trees and surrounding brush. The call of the *chicharra grande* had overtaken their ears, but the horses and the dog felt and heard something else within their wild song. The horses' ears continued to point at the same group of trees. And they were still desperately trying to pull away.

"Go check it out, Juarez," Cooper said to the agent standing in front of them.

Juarez turned back and looked up at him. "Check out what? It's just the cicadas humming!"

"No way. *Chicharras* don't scare my horse. It's not bugs," Ruiz insisted.

"You check it out," Juarez suggested to Ruiz.

Ruiz pulled out an LED flashlight and pointed it into the humid air in front of them. There was a group of trees only thirty feet away from them in the darkness. He shined the light into the brush on the ground and then pointed it into the leaves hanging down from the desert trees. Nothing. Then the sounds from the annoying bugs suddenly stopped.

Talamantez was pulled abruptly by his dog. "She's freaking out!"

"Go take a look, Juarez!" Ruiz hissed, breaking the silence.

Agent Juarez lifted his head and grabbed the flashlight from his belt. Sweat dripped from underneath his hat. With each step forward, his olive green uniform swished against itself in the eerie silence. The other agents and the two men they had captured now watched as Agent Ricardo Juarez moved in closer toward the disturbance in the group of thorny mesquite trees and brush—the disturbance that only their animals seemed to be able to sense.

A snap.

Juarez halted and reached as if to draw his weapon, but called out into the brush instead. "United States Border Patrol! *Venga aqui!*"

Nothing.

He tried his flashlight again and proceeded to step closer to the trees, his hand hovering over his holster. "*Venga aqui!*"

A few steps further and his face was practically against a tree. He drew his weapon slowly and listened. He could hear a strange sound now, and there was a putrid, sour smell. He squinted his eyes and scanned the brush, bending at the knees and tilting his head to see around the jagged tree before him.

One of the horses let out a loud and forceful snort. He could feel something near him. Juarez turned his head to the left and steadied his gun, aiming it upward and into the nothingness of leaves that were now rustling.

Eyes.

They were on top of him. Above his head. Taller than he was, its shoulders and arms were larger than he could believe. The eyes were shining like ice—grayish-blue ... and they looked angry.

"Oh, God!" Juarez breathed out. His heartbeat was out of control.

There was a deep growling sound that emanated from the thing as it rose and stood taller to reveal itself from within the brush. It continued to stand higher and grow in size until it stood to look down on him. It was a thing of nightmares that was not supposed to exist.

It's not real, Juarez prayed silently. His body shook. It couldn't be true.

It flashed its fangs and opened its large mouth. Juarez reacted by firing a shot at it, sinking a bullet into its arm. The creature in the brush then let out a deep roar before swiping its massive claws across the agent's chest, ripping through his uniform and forcing him to the ground in agony.

Just feet away, Cooper's horse reacted by throwing him off and escaping into the desert.

The creature that had attacked Juarez then disappeared into the night on all fours at a speed the men could not calculate or understand. The canine agent steadied his dog enough to draw his weapon to fire upon the creature, but missed. He then rushed over to assist Agent Juarez. Blood gushed from the agent's body. The deep gashes began at his neck and ended at his hips.

The captured illegals stood and took cover behind Agent Ruiz as he worked to calm his horse. Sensing the intensity of their fear and feeling responsible for their safety, he looked back to check on the men hiding behind him before calling out to Talamantez, "Is he all right?"

"No! I've called EMS!" Agent Talamantez's voice quivered as if he was now sobbing. "He's been … ripped apart!"

"*Lobo!*" The older of the two illegals cried out.

Cooper turned to him from where he had landed after being thrown by his horse. "What?"

"*Lobo.*" His body shook uncontrollably. "*La maldición. Como en Inglés?*"

"Wolf curse," the other man interpreted for him.

Agent Nikolas Vaughn had been connected immediately with a representative from the Border Patrol. It was late. The woman on the phone didn't seem very irritated or put out by it though. Nikolas knew that if his contact had been selected to deal with the issue, she had to know that it was something serious.

"Did shifts just begin or are they changing soon?" Agent Vaughn asked the woman.

"Uh … yeah." She rubbed on her forehead and eye, and considered making a cup of coffee. "They're changing shifts about now. The next shift should be getting out of muster and heading out into the field," she responded groggily while checking the time on the oven. She felt blank and confused. She had just received a call from Washington D.C. and was told that she was going to be dealing with a high-priority situation. She was then asked if she had been sleeping. After she answered, "no" she was instructed to relocate to someplace private within her home. Her call was then connected to another call. Top Secret. She was told to give the man on the phone all of her cooperation and any available resources, if requested. This was to be carried out as quietly as possible.

"That's not good," Agent Vaughn sighed. "I need *less* people out there. Not more."

"What can I do to help you, sir. I don't know the situation, but if I can assist you in any way …"

"I need you to alter that report about the large bear." Agent Vaughn paused to think for a moment.

What report? "Yes, sir." The woman now knew to go ahead and make that coffee.

"And I need the report to include something about prior descriptions from witnesses being inaccurate … misidentified."

"Yes, sir."

"I need a truck with a cage in the back," the man instructed.

"For human transport?"

"Yes. And I need a few of your agents. The best you've got. With tasers, GPS, NVGs … just two agents."

"Okay … and where should I have them meet you?" The woman was wishing she had never been tapped as an intelligence contact. A bear could not be the cause of this much commotion.

"I am in a black Tahoe and will be heading out for the industrial area near the fence. I was told there's a shoe factory near there. We'll use that as a meeting point."

"Yes, sir."

"Have your agents there in two trucks in about five minutes."

"Uh … five minutes? I will do my best to …"

"And do *not* forget that bear report. Get it out to your agents now. Tell them that it has a disease. Tell them it's crazed."

Good Lord, what's happening out there? "Right away, sir."

Ten minutes later, Agent Juarez was in the back of an ambulance, in shock and fighting for his life from wounds that none of the EMTs had ever seen before.

30

Edward and Deidra waited outside their vehicle as Nikolas briefed the two military policemen. Nikolas knew the game well. He was going to keep the two camouflaged men as informed and involved as they needed to be. They had parked their SUVs just outside the entrance of the shoe factory and waited. Martin sat a few feet away, half inside and half outside of an Air Force SUV, with Vincent slumped over and snoring next to him.

Edward watched as Martin began to run his fingers over his slicked-out hair. "Your brother is like … Elvis. A cool … priest Elvis."

"They should have been here already," Deidra complained while kicking at the rocks on the ground. "It's freakin' hot out here."

"Shouldn't we be in one car or something by now? Vincent is knocked out. I don't think he's going to attack us," Edward said.

"Let's ask Nik. I'm sure there's a reason we're all separated like this."

Edward looked at her with a smirk across his face. "What do we need to ask him for?" He crossed his arms and turned to face her. His features were stern. "Why is a *cook* running this show?"

"He knows people," Deidra explained.

"Yeah, I get it. But why are all of these government people listening to some motorcycle club guy? Think about it."

"He has connections." She looked Edward over, knowing that he had to be sweltering in the suit jacket he insisted on wearing for the trip. Edward knew that he would be meeting with various city and government officials in Del Rio, and it had him on edge before they had even left his house. She tried to convince him to wear a polo instead and suggested that he relax. One day he would know that he had nothing to prove to these people.

"Why are you defending him?" Edward spat with hatred.

Deidra pulled back from him. The look in her eyes pierced Edward as he instantly regretted his words. Martin moved in closer and shot Nikolas a look of caution as he approached them.

"You guys doing okay?" Nikolas asked.

"Yes, everything is fine," Deidra answered.

"Those Border Patrol agents should be here any minute. We'll follow the last sighting and—"

"I have a problem with all of this," Edward cut Nikolas off to announce.

"A problem with what, sir?" Nikolas asked.

"A problem with *you*." Edward stepped closer to Nikolas and was breathing hard from his nose. His mouth was twisted in anger.

Deidra could hardly believe the tone in Edward's voice.

"Well, what's the problem?" Nikolas asked calmly, holding on to his composure but standing taller to display some confidence.

Edward stared into his eyes as if challenging him to back away. "You haven't been talking to us about any of this shit that's going on. You're just calling secret contacts on your damn phone. I'm supposed to believe that you have all of this taken care of?"

"Yes, you are," Nikolas replied.

Edward turned back to face Deidra. "Why the hell are we even out here? He's already taking care of it all by himself." The sarcasm was harsh and thick.

"Edward!" Deidra yelled. "Whatever is going on here is connected to Vinny! Stop fucking around! We'll talk about this later! Let Nik take care of—"

"Take care of what?!" Edward pressed on. "A plate of spaghetti?" He turned back to face Nikolas for a reaction.

There was only a stone-faced glare.

The two military policemen moved in a little closer so they could listen.

"Edward!" Deidra yelled and pulled on Edward's sleeve, yanking him to the side. She positioned herself between the two of them. "Nik, I'm sorry ..."

"Yeah, Deidra! You're sorry for what?" Edward's eyes were filled with rage. "Because you're still in love with him or because he's nothing but a punk gang leader that we have put all of our trust into?!"

"Edward!" she screamed. "I can't believe you would do this right now!"

"Mr. Bloodgood," Nikolas began. "I'm not here to overstep my boundaries in any way. Congressman Montemayor is partially my responsibility, and I'm taking care of it. You decided to come out here. I understand that Montemayor has financial ties to The Society. You should be thanking me for helping you."

Edward pushed past Deidra and grabbed ahold of Nikolas's shirt collar, pulling his face down closer to his own.

Nikolas tensed up and prepared himself to reach for his weapon.

Deidra noticed. "No!" she pleaded.

Edward sneered into Nikolas's face. The perfect scruffiness of his stubble aggravated him. His stylish tattoos and confident demeanor had become increasingly annoying. There was something wrong with this perfect man, and he was certain that Deidra, as distrusting as she usually was, was now absolutely blind to it. But it was becoming more obvious to Edward by the minute. "I don't trust you. After this is done, I don't want to see or hear from you ever again. Do you understand?"

"Let go of me."

"Or what? You'll shoot me? Go ahead," Edward dared him.

"Nik! No … Edward, let him go!" Deidra said to them frantically.

"I couldn't shoot you even if I wanted to, … *sir*," Nikolas said quietly.

"Why not?"

"Because I've been ordered to help watch you."

Edward loosened his grip. "What are you talking about?"

Behind them, two Border Patrol trucks pulled up.

"Let go of me," Nikolas warned.

"Ordered to watch me?" Edward repeated back to him. "What are you talking about?"

"Let him go," Deidra begged quietly, feeling the eyes of everyone around them staring. She worked her way back in between them again. She gently pulled Edward closer to her and got an arm around his waist. She walked him toward her brother, who was standing by and ready to assist her with Edward.

Edward let his posture sink into himself. He dragged his feet as Deidra led him further away from the embarrassing scene he had created. He braced himself to face her disapproval.

"What is wrong with you? We're chasing a fucking werewolf that's about to cross into Mexico and cause some international incident. We're dragging a guy along with us that we've drugged in order to prevent him from going full-alien on us. … There's cops everywhere. … The military is involved now—and the feds! Why are you doing this?"

He hung his head low. "I don't know."

"Edward, this is not the time to freak out on Nik. He's been helping us. Montemayor is connected to The Society. We have to find him and figure out what is going on before he fucks it all up for us!" she scolded him.

"Deidra," Edward spoke in a hoarse whisper that made his voice crack. "I … I feel … I need to tell you something."

Deidra looked behind Edward to catch the look in her brother's eyes. When she did, her brother nodded his head toward Edward, signaling to her that he was obviously trying to tell her something important. "Okay, look. We can talk about whatever it is later."

I love you. "Okay," he agreed.

The military policemen started walking toward their SUVs as Nikolas greeted the Border Patrol agents and relayed to them some brief instructions. He also worked to play down the near-fight the agents had witnessed when they pulled up, explaining to them that the guy in the suit wasn't taking too well to the extreme heat. That, and it had probably been a while since he had gotten laid.

Hesitantly, Nikolas then returned to Edward and Deidra. The Border Patrol agents had given him an update on their situation. "We have to go. Those agents just told me that there's been another sighting. He attacked one of their agents. We need to try and trap him somehow."

Edward picked up his head and faced him. "I'm sorry, Nik. Thanks for all of your help."

"I'll remember to take it out on you later. Let's go," Nikolas answered back.

"Uh …" Edward looked at Deidra. "Is he kidding?"

"He doesn't joke around too much. I'm sure the spaghetti comment didn't help. Get in and wait for me." She pointed to the dark blue military vehicle. "I'll be right back."

He wanted to explain to her how stupid he felt for losing control of his emotions and hoped that he hadn't distanced her. He wondered if she felt repulsed at the thought of sitting next to him now. She was probably going to ask around for another ride.

He watched her follow Nikolas to the Tahoe. Edward got into the back of the SUV and heaved a heavy sigh. He wanted more than anything at that moment to take back what he had said to Nikolas and save it for another time. Maybe a time when a group of armed feds and a priest weren't around to watch him make a fool of himself. Maybe when they weren't chasing a werewolf on the Mexican border. The more he thought about it, there were probably an infinite number of better times to confront Nik. *Everything I do sucks.*

"Nik?" Deidra asked. He sat in the driver's seat of the Tahoe and started fumbling with a handheld GPS. He was turned in his seat toward her.

"Yes?" he answered without looking up.

"Edward is right. I mean, he said it all stupid and without thinking it through, but ..."

"And he was insulting."

"Yes. That too. Look, I know you have connections in high places, but this is getting a little weird. It's almost ... unbelievable."

He set the GPS on the dashboard and tilted his head to look at her. "I tried to tell you why I left the department. You didn't want to hear it."

"When did you try to tell me?"

"Several times."

Silence. She thought about it.

Nikolas looked her over gently and then looked away as if in pain. "Your mother's murder was one of the worst things I have ever dealt with."

Deidra bit the inside of her lip as she decided to keep quiet and listen to him. No matter how painful it got.

"There's too much evil out there. I took ... a government job. They call me when they need me. I'm hoping it might help me get where I want to be with the Knights. But for right now, I can't do it all on my own. Maybe one day I can. Maybe one day, I'll have the same liberty that Edward does."

Deidra was afraid to ask, but had to. "Which agency did you sign up with?"

Nikolas hesitated in answering. He wanted to share his world with her without holding back. The pull on his conscience was in her direction, but there was too much to explain and they didn't have the time. "The one that approached me and asked for my help. They made a pretty good case."

"Nik." She frowned. "Tell me."

"We have to go, Deidra. Maybe we can talk about it another time. Over dinner."

"Well …"

"We're following the last sighting we heard on the radio. So, that's our next step. We have to go now," he added quickly to prevent her from turning him down.

"Alright," she agreed with worry in her eyes. Even if she wasn't ready to completely trust anyone, she was going to trust Nikolas … for now. He had seen the creature. He had watched it change into the thing that was now loose on the border between Texas and Mexico. At least, that's where they hoped it still was.

She ran to join Edward inside the military SUV as each of them got into formation to follow Nikolas on their quest to capture a werewolf.

31

"The radio room just put out a sensor activation near Amistad Dam," one of the Border Patrol agents informed Nikolas through the window of his truck. They were stopped alongside a desolate-looking road. Nikolas was pulled up next to the agent's truck with the other agent stopped just ahead of them.

"Get the coordinates and we'll follow you," Nikolas instructed through his passenger side window. "Make sure we are the only ones to respond."

"Yes, sir."

As the agent performed a dusty turn-around on the narrow road, Nikolas decided to call Edward about their plan. There had been quite a lot of talk about capturing and not much on what to do once they closed in on the beast. He would respectfully call Edward and leave the decision making to him.

"Yes?" Edward answered as their driver started turning them back in the direction they had just come from.

"Sir, we need a plan for capturing Montemayor. We're turning around because we may have located him."

Edward worked to fight past the embarrassment from earlier. He still wasn't able to look at Deidra, except for a few stolen glances out of the corner of his eye. And now he was expected to devise some plan out of thin air for capturing something he only thought to exist in legend. "Okay."

"So, tell me what you think we should do? We're headed toward the dam. We should be there in minutes." Nikolas doubted him.

This must be his revenge for the spaghetti comment. "I think ..." Edward scrambled up a plan as he spoke. "Deidra said something about exorcisms and werewolves. We can pull up on him and have Martin get out ... I guess ... and try to talk to him. To Montemayor."

Nikolas thought on it before speaking. "Uh ... the only problem is that he could run away or viciously attack. One of the two. We don't know how much of a werewolf he is or if that's really what he is at all. I'm not completely convinced. It's not even a full moon tonight."

Edward banged his head on the window when he attempted to search the sky for the moon. "Ow."

"I would suggest we get a tranquilizer gun from the Parks and Wildlife guys, but I worry about the effects it might have on him since we aren't too sure ... what he is," Nikolas continued.

"We have tons of morphine!" Edward remembered.

"Full moon stuff is all bull," Deidra said without turning to look at Edward.

"The full moon stuff is bull," Edward relayed into the phone.

"Yeah, I heard."

"We can get Martin to grab a dose of morphine out of the supply we brought for Vincent, have him carefully approach Montemayor and, if he attacks, Martin can stick him with a needle," Edward said with hesitant enthusiasm.

"It's a huge risk. Has Vincent been doing okay with his dosage? We wouldn't even know how much to give a seven-foot werewolf."

Deidra leaned over to add something to the conversation. "We give Vincent a large dose because of his condition. Something about him causes the drug to wear off faster. Maybe try Vincent's dosage."

Nikolas sighed. "I don't know."

"What if he bites Martin?" Deidra asked, suddenly realizing something as she looked at the phone in Edward's hand.

Edward looked at her inquisitively. "That part's true? Would Martin turn into a werewolf if it bites him?"

"I don't know." She shrugged her shoulders. "But I don't think Martin will like taking that chance. Do you?"

Edward had an idea. "We can have the military guys and those agents covering him. We don't have silver bullets but—"

"Silver bullets are Hollywood," Deidra chimed in for both Edward and Nikolas to hear. "It's all a lie."

"Okay," Edward continued. He pulled the phone away from his ear and held it in the air closer to Deidra. "Either way, at least the bullets might hurt him enough to make him back off of Martin."

"And they might give us enough time to inject him with more of the drug if the first dose isn't enough—if it comes to that," Deidra added.

"Shit." Edward realized that he was volunteering Martin for a job that no one in their right mind would volunteer for. "Well, all we can do is ask him if he'll do it, right, Nik?"

"I agree. I'll call him," Nikolas offered before remembering where he wanted to stand with Edward. "Unless you wanted to ask him yourself."

"No, go ahead," Edward replied. "But, what do we do with Montemayor once we have him?"

"We get him to a church," Deidra brushed the hair from her face.

"We'll have to find one first and then what? Break in?" Edward asked her.

"I already found one on my phone, and yes, if it's not open, we break in. But I think Martin can take care of having it ready for us when we arrive," she replied with full confidence in her voice.

"I'll call Martin," Nikolas said before disconnecting.

Edward stared at Deidra's profile with his hand against his chin. He opened his mouth a few times, but the words were stuck inside his head.

"What?" she asked him.

"Won't it look a little obvious if we have all of these government trucks parked in front of a church and we drag some wolfman and a ... crazy alien-possessed guy inside?"

"It will be fine."

"Why a church? For the exorcism?" he asked.

"Yes. I'm kinda hoping to get Martin into it a little more. You know, like setting the mood. He's having a hard time believing any of this."

"Seriously? That's why you want all of us at a church?" Edward couldn't believe what he was hearing. "Is this like setting up a school play to you?"

"No. A church setting might inspire him. I need him to take care of both of them at once. Martin doesn't get it ... Vincent still needs an exorcism. Maybe with the wolfman, we can get a two-for-one deal."

"Jesus," Edward shook his head in amazement. When it came to her mind's logic and reasoning powers, there seemed to be a malfunction of sorts. Her scams somehow seemed to work most of the time, but the days and minutes leading up to their fruition always drove him into a state of serious panic. "What if he says no?"

"He can't!" She spun around in her seat to face him as fast as her seatbelt would let her. "Do you want to put up with this crazy Vincent stuff any longer?!"

"No."

"Of course you don't! And you have the power to make sure that Martin says some prayers and flicks some holy water on Vincent to make it all stop."

"But, he said he isn't possessed ..."

"I know! But he doesn't know anything about aliens! Vincent believes in the Church and its powers. Vincent's mind can push the alien, or whatever the aliens did to him, out of his mind." Deidra sounded exasperated with explaining things to everyone. "But he needs Martin's help to do it. He needs to feel like he is being cleansed. Martin is being difficult. You need to force him to do it!"

"How am I supposed to do that? I'm not going to bully a priest!"

"Tell him you care about me and that you just want him to do it to make me feel better. Make him feel like he's right about Vinny, but just ... get him to humor me, okay?"

She's so beautiful. "Okay," he relented.

She lowered her voice before speaking so the driver would not hear. "Screw those aliens. Trying to steal our racers." She crossed her arms and stared out into the desert of Val Verde County. The world's many forms of evil and corruption were on her mind.

Edward wondered something fearfully to himself and then decided to ask. He lowered his voice. "Won't the greys be pissed off at us if we help Vincent?"

"Maybe," she confessed without emotion. "But we don't even know which group did this to him. It could have been the greys we work with, one of their rebel groups, or the ... never mind."

"So you're willing to take the risk?"

"Yes. Vinny's a part of our club. Whatever or whoever did this to him, it isn't right. He's just ... a kid. Someone's son. He didn't deserve this. And I'm getting tired of it. We're always the ones taking orders from them. Maybe ... we should be standing up for ourselves more often." The pressures of keeping *them* happy always seemed to cling to her.

"Is there something more to this than you're telling me?" It didn't feel right. He knew how intimidated she was when it came to The Society's alien relations. That, and there was anger in her voice. She looked betrayed. It was in her eyes.

She leaned in closer to him and reached for his wrist, turning it in her direction to pretend to read the time on it. She was certain that their drivers were not just assigned to them without the expected intelligence-gathering instructions that went along with the job. But unfortunately, they needed their help. The official-looking uniforms and government vehicles did impress and intimidate, when needed. They also added to their armament. She spoke as close to his ear as she possibly could without drawing any attention from the driver. "I'm pretty sure the racer-stealing thing is a front."

Edward had learned quickly in the game when to play along. "My watch is slow." He smiled at her and then lifted his eyebrows so she would continue.

"From the rumors I have heard, I think they're testing something on Vinny ..." She could see the eyes of the driver glance at them through the rear view mirror.

Edward noticed it also. "I just wear it for decoration ..."

"... to use on the general population. Or just a selected, chosen part of the population."

Edward couldn't hold it in. "Why?"

Her face grew dark and serious for a moment, but she forced herself to swallow back the pain of her words. "For a possible relocation project." Her eyes studied his and then looked back down to the watch again. "I like your watch. You have good taste in accessories. Of course, I had to teach you to appreciate good taste."

He reached for her hand and lightly squeezed it, while doing everything in his power to keep from thinking about the chilling vision she had placed into his head. He pushed away the images of humans being forced to live on other planets, for whatever insane reasons that the aliens might have, and instead focused in on the way her satin hair was draped against his shoulder. He then realized that the relocation of humans to other planets may have been part of a contingency plan—not one to harm them, but to help *save* the human race. He knew that Deidra wasn't optimistic enough to consider that possibility. But, it crossed his mind. Visions of the apocalypse rushed through him. Maybe Vincent was simply a pawn in a dangerous game played by angry investors seeking revenge over lost profits. Or, maybe he was part of a serious test. A test meant to save us in the event of an unforeseen catastrophe. Human survival could be on the line. Relocation ... the Earth could be in danger. Perhaps something horrible actually *was* going to happen to their planet—or maybe Deidra's paranoia was just getting worse. Perhaps it was nothing more than an elaborate delusion. *She is filled with distrust and has no one to comfort her.* He pulled her hand closer to him, dismissing all doubt in her reaction to his doing so, and she did not resist.

32

"They have it on night vision. I have the coordinates," the agent said to Nikolas from the driver's seat of his truck.

"Good. Let's make sure we don't have any patrol in the area, and we need to divert any searches from the air," Nikolas replied through his passenger side window. When the two green and white trucks ahead of him pulled over again, he knew something was up. They were getting closer. Hopefully the beast had not crossed into Mexico.

"Yes, sir. I'll inform my supervisor immediately. The animal appears to be steady at one location now. Did you want us to move in?"

"Make that call to clear out the area. Then we'll move in."

"Yes, sir."

As the Border Patrol agent got on his phone, Nikolas did the same, and checked his text messages. He had received a message from Deidra. It read, "Is Martin ready to do this?"

Nikolas typed back, "He says he is."

"He doesn't believe it though."

"He will be fine."

Deidra let out a tense breath before she decided to call Martin for herself. After their convoy took to the road again, they started driving over some rugged terrain, which made text messages a challenge to compose. Texts couldn't adequately convey the seriousness of the situation anyway.

"Hello, Sissy," Martin answered with a smile. "How are you?"

"Martin, do you have the syringes ready?"

"I have one prepared."

"You will need more than one," she emphasized her words with care. Having constantly been accused of being the overly dramatic sister had changed her style of communication with him.

"I think two doses might hurt the man."

He's not going to listen. Deidra closed her eyes. "He's not a man. In his unnatural state, a human dosage may not be enough to subdue him."

"Deidra," Martin answered back, "I was told that he was probably shot, okay? And Nik told me that they aren't reporting any movement. So, I don't think there will be much of a fight coming from him. He sounds tired and weak."

"Martin, you need to be ready for anything to happen!"

"You want me to coax him into one of the agent's trucks with promises that I can help him, right?" he asked as if leading up to a point.

"Yes, but—"

"If he tries to … scratch or bite me … I stick him with the needle, right?"

"Yes, but—"

"It will be fine. Don't worry." Martin looked over at Vincent—sleeping hard next to him. "And you know what? Vincent hasn't been that bad. He only woke up once and called me a mother fucker, but then he went right back to sleep." Martin smiled.

"That's great, Martin." Deidra looked at Edward and rolled her eyes. "Good luck with the humongous werewolf. If you don't make it, I'll have your body cremated and scatter your ashes at sea, just like you asked."

"No, I never said th—"

Deidra ended the call and eyed Edward. He was fidgeting nervously with his seatbelt, repeatedly pulling it outward and then releasing it so that it would snap back onto his chest. "That's annoying."

"Is your brother going to be able to handle this?"

She studied the concern on his face. He was tired. There were lines on his forehead and puffiness around his eyes. "I think once he sees … it, instinct will kick in. I hope."

Their approach over the rocky landscape that made up the west Texas desert was a generic experience for Deidra. She had seen it before and felt it to be fraught with cliché and sadness. For personal reasons, she had already made up her mind to hate it. But from their parked spot on a small cactus-infested hill, the way the moonlight reflected with a rippling motion on the Rio Grande River was mesmerizing.

Nikolas tapped lightly on Edward's window, startling Deidra. Edward let the window down to greet him. "He's close?"

"Yes. I think we should reorganize into just two vehicles before getting any closer."

"Good idea."

Nikolas leaned in just enough to address them both. "Is it okay if I ride with you guys?"

"Of course," Edward answered.

They traveled from the hill and through the rugged terrain, using the light of the moon and GPS coordinates to guide them. Their headlights were off. Packed into two vehicles, Martin rode with the two Border Patrol agents in one of their trucks. One of the MP's was told to stay behind with Vincent, who was snoring away in the back of his vehicle.

"So you're sure the moon has nothing to do with it?" Edward asked a worried-looking Deidra. He knew to keep his voice down.

They were moving at a crawl. Nikolas and their driver were both now wearing a night vision goggle on one eye. They were silent and leaned forward in their seats.

"I've never dealt with this kind of thing before, but in the legends I have studied, no, the moon isn't really a factor. The whole werewolf concept-thing appeared in ancient Roman lore. It could even go back to the ancient Egyptians or the Sumerians," Deidra explained with a pensive frown. "Besides, it looks more like a gibbous moon out there tonight."

"A what?" Edward asked.

She turned and smiled. "A most-moon."

"Oh ... right," he answered stupidly.

Deidra returned to peering out her window. She did this with nothing in her eyes but the basest of fear. Edward's discomfort with this pierced him deeply, causing him to conduct his own search through the brush and trees surrounding them as well.

"Ancient Romans?" Nikolas asked.

Deidra stopped scanning through the darkness outside her window to think for a moment before answering back. It would have seemed more fitting to speak of such things in front of a campfire. But unlike playful stories, she wasn't trying to frighten them. She was warning them. "Lupercus. The Roman god. There was a festival held for him. The Wolf Festival. Later on, it came to be known as, or replaced by, Valentine's Day."

"Really?" Edward asked.

"Yes. But also, the story of a curse may have originated from it as well ... or at least the legend surrounding a curse," she sighed.

"And the Egyptian connection?" Nikolas asked.

"Well, that's a simple one." Deidra went back to gazing out her window again. "Anubis."

"The jackal-headed god?" Edward seemed more surprised than Nikolas.

"Some academics believe that Anubis was misidentified as having the head of a jackal when, in fact, he may have had the head of an African gray wolf instead."

"The truck in front of us is stopping," their driver informed them with a clear and professional tone. He was certain that their talk of legend and myth was just that. Being assigned to escort this group felt more like a joke with each passing minute. Top Secret clearance wasted. The lack of luster in the mission had become a disappointment. He now wondered how much he should embellish things in his report in order to impress his superiors.

Nikolas quickly answered an incoming call. "Yes? Okay ... that close? ... Yes. Be ready to cover him. We'll be ready on our side. Okay. Proceed."

When he ended his conversation with the agent from the truck in front of them, Nikolas turned back to Edward and stared blankly. For the first time since meeting Nikolas, Edward sensed a true fear escaping from the look in his eyes. "They are going to move in a little closer and then step out on foot with Martin."

"Okay," Edward replied.

"We'll stay back a bit and be ready to move in if we need to." Nikolas eyed the driver next to him and watched as he crept their vehicle closely behind the green and white truck guiding them. "You might have to use that weapon of yours," Nikolas warned him.

"Yes, sir."

"Deidra?" Nikolas called back.

"Yes, I'm carrying a Beretta," she responded automatically.

Nikolas then pulled the gun from his shoulder holster and studied it. He tilted the Walther in his hand a few times at different angles as if searching it for some magical button that might help him in fighting off the unknown. The nine-millimeter felt worthless in his hand. "What are you carrying, Sergeant?"

"An M-4 and an M-9, sir."

"Security forces training won't be enough for this one, Sergeant," Nikolas warned him. "When we stop and exit, have the M-4 ready, but do everything in your power not to use it. Keep it for show unless I give the order."

"Yes, sir."

Their vehicle then made an abrupt stop.

Nikolas looked ahead and watched as one of the Border Patrol agents exited from the driver's seat and quickly stepped into position to aim his weapon over the hood of his truck.

"Even if I fire, wait for my order ... unless I am hurt and cannot give the order," Nikolas reminded him, his eyes fixated on the passenger side door opening on the truck in front of them. The bottom part of Martin's cassock was now beginning to emerge.

"Yes, sir."

Deidra and Edward scooted up closer to Nikolas and watched through the windshield in awe as Martin stepped out onto the rocky terrain in his polished black loafers. It felt dreamlike and surreal. And before either of them could say a word, Nikolas and the military sergeant had nodded in silent agreement to follow.

"Jesus," Deidra whispered to Edward while gripping the back of the now empty seat in front of her. She watched as Nikolas held his weapon ready and maneuvered his way through the twists of cacti and crooked trees in the darkness surrounding them. The sergeant followed close behind him, giving her only a partial sense of peace, but not enough. "I should go with th—"

But before she could finish her sentence, Edward had pushed his door open with a soft click and was crouched down and headed toward the truck parked in front of them with a semi-tiptoe in his step and a Beretta in his hands.

"Dammit, Eddie!"

33

Several yards ahead, lying curled up in the sandy soil next to the river, was the monstrous creature. Nikolas and an agent could see it in their night vision goggles, heaving in quickened breaths while on its side. It faced the opposite direction and seemed to be unaware of their presence, although Nikolas didn't understand how that could be possible. Its senses had to be ten times stronger than that of a normal animal and yet it didn't react to them.

Edward was careful to stay back as Nikolas and Martin assessed their next course of action. He looked at the gun in his hand a few times and decided to let it hang loosely at his side as if he was in control of what he was doing. Martin looked back at him as Nikolas used his free hand to emphasize something important as he spoke. Martin took on the paleness of a ghost, and he bit on his lip.

Edward walked up to the men gathered by the truck. Nikolas handed his night vision monocular to Martin and helped to point it in the right direction.

"… and you can see if he responds to that before asking him to come with us. We don't have much time. We'll have to move in quickly," Nikolas was explaining to him.

Martin's jaw quivered before answering. His mouth gaped open as he focused through the lens. "So you'll call out his name first, right? To see if he reacts to it ... like a human?"

"Yes. That's all we're trying to do. Reach his human side," Nikolas said. "We'll make our move based on his reaction."

"Do you want this?" Edward cut in, holding up the gun in his hand.

Martin lowered the monocular and turned to him. "No ... no ... that's alright," he answered.

"We'll be covering him," Nikolas assured Edward. "He has to concentrate on using the morphine if he has to."

"Okay." Edward looked up at Martin. "Are you ready for this?"

"Not really." Martin held up the special monocular, offering it to Edward. "He's ... *real*. Did you want to see?" His hand shook and his voice was unsteady.

Edward took ahold of the goggle and aimed it toward the part of the river Martin was being prepared to approach. Martin, Nikolas, and the military policeman began to make their way down from the small cliff just as Edward spotted the creature they were headed toward. "Oh ... man."

Its fur appeared lighter than Edward had expected, but he then realized that it had to be from the effect of seeing it in night vision. Because of the position it was lying in, he could see the pads of its large feet, twitching and full of claws. A bushy tail flicked slowly behind it on the ground. It was very clear to him how huge this thing was. Its muscular presence, even as it appeared to sleep, filled his imagination with fearful scenarios. "Aren't we going with them?" he asked the agents that had stayed behind.

"We'll move in if we have to," one answered back, also watching through a monocular that was attached to black headgear strapped around his head and face.

"They should be pretty close," the other agent said to his partner.

"They are. The priest is moving in."

Martin grabbed some of the black material around his knee and held it up as he crouched down. He was only about twenty feet away from the crumpled up beast. The pattern of its breathing had increased. It seemed to be aware of their presence but afraid to turn around to face them—whatever they were. They were a threat.

Martin took only one step closer to it before turning his head back to check that Nikolas was still positioned close by. He was aimed and ready on the nightmare ahead that was lying next to the river in a scattering of brush and cane. Martin waved at Nikolas with fear in his eyes. "Now!" he mouthed in exaggeration through the silence and thick humidity between them.

Nikolas breathed in and hoped for the best. "Fernando!" he called out and waited a few seconds before trying again. "Fernando, it's Nik. Fernando, we know you are injured. We want to help you."

The only sound that could be heard breaking through the moistened air was the song of many cicadas humming together in the trees. The creature remained still except for the awkward, fast-paced breathing. Martin looked back to Nikolas again and frantically pointed at himself.

Nikolas immediately took the cue. "We have a priest, Fernando! He can make this go away! All you have to do is turn around and get up slowly. We just want to help!"

The creature's rate of breathing increased but with short stops in between panicked sets. It had heard him. Whether it was able to understand or not, Nikolas was now certain that it was too weakened to attack. Through the greenish tint of the night vision goggle, he could gauge by the creature's reaction to them—its change in breathing—that it was in a state of pure terror.

"My name is Father Bonaparte," Martin began. "I have come to pray over you and to remove the curse from your body. If you are hurt, we can help you with that, too." He crossed himself and trembled before continuing. "Please. Turn around. Give us a sign that you will come with us. You are in danger. Others are working to hunt you down. Please come with us."

The creature brought its arm up slowly and held it into the air. Its fingers spread out to reveal enormous, menacing claws. It tilted its body in an attempt to face them—to acknowledge the voices, but it stopped suddenly and winced, almost howl-like, in tremendous pain. Its profile could now be seen. Martin gasped in shock and stepped backward on himself, falling into the rocks beneath him.

Nikolas and the Air Force sergeant both steadied their aim as they watched it through their goggles. More of a wolf than a man, it opened its snout and panted hard. Its bushy tail stopped moving, and its pointed ears stood up in an attempt to focus in on the men nearby. From the gaping mouth, a display of large, sharp fangs appeared. The hair covering its body was coarse and a mixture of medium to light gray in color. And on its bicep and shoulder was blood from a gunshot wound that had soaked its fur.

From where he sat shaking, Martin made his plea once again. "Fernando, let me come closer to you. I know you are in pain." Martin rose slowly to regain his footing. "I have something to take the pain away."

Fernando let his arm fall limp to his side and he made the effort again to turn his body toward them. With the twisting of his torso, he whimpered like a dog. The high-pitched cry of pain caused Martin to flinch sympathetically. He watched as Fernando used his good arm to support and lift himself onto his knees. Moments after he was steady, Fernando let his head hang in defeat, only lifting his eyes to gaze desperately at the priest.

"Yes," Martin encouraged him. "That's good. Can you come closer?"

Fernando's good arm shook uncontrollably as it almost gave out on him.

Martin held up the medical needle in his hand so that Fernando could see. "I'm just going to give you an injection. It's to help with the pain."

Fernando forced himself to crawl closer as agonizing pain seared through him. He dragged his body toward the priest; he could see the needle waiting for him, and the guns pointed in his direction. Everything around him had become a blur, but he knew that the needle would help.

"Fernando, let me approach you. I can meet you halfway," Martin offered. He was only about ten feet from him now.

Fernando held his head up higher and slowly blinked his eyes. He swayed back and forth, fragile and exhausted. "Help ... pain," the deep, throaty voice begged with vocal cords that sounded unnatural and torn.

My God, Martin thought to himself. He quickly approached the werewolf, knelt on one knee, and cautiously placed the needle in Fernando's forearm, allowing the drug to enter his veins. Fernando sighed and slumped onto the ground in front of Martin, landing partly on his shoe and on the hemline of his cassock. The werewolf's crisp, icy gray eyes locked onto Martin's face and searched it for solace and hope. The gunshot wound on his bicep was worse than Martin had expected for such an enormous creature.

"Close your eyes, Fernando," Martin urged him. He caressed the top of Fernando's head, not knowing where the courage came from to do so. He could hear the footsteps of men coming up behind them. "They are going to help carry you. We are going to a church where it will be safe to ... remove the curse."

Fernando nodded his head slowly. Nikolas walked up and lowered himself down next to Martin to get a better look at Fernando's condition in the moonlight.

"You did great, Martin," Nikolas stared into the pale, glassy eyes looking up at him from the ground and then forced himself to focus instead on the ghastly wound on Fernando's arm. He did his best to push personal feelings aside. "We might need to get another dose into him soon. It may not be enough for his size."

"You are probably right," Martin responded softly.

"The truck is pulling up closer. It should only take about fifteen minutes to get to that church."

Fernando grunted and his eyelids flickered as he arched his back in pain. "Kill me," he wheezed in that deep raspy voice.

"God," Nikolas exhaled, with his eyes widened. It was unexpected. Nothing about that voice sounded like Fernando and it stunned him. His friend was now an abomination. It had seriously wounded a federal agent and Nikolas was certain that, as Congressman Montemayor, Fernando had something to do with the disappearance of a woman in San Antonio. He could see the human part of him someplace within the eyes, but it was more of a tortured animal now than a man. Its ungodly vocal pitch clung to him—dark and unfathomable to the human ear.

Fernando placed his hand on top of his chest and peered into Nikolas's eyes. Familiar and safe, the boy he had watched become a man had been kind enough to bring him a savior priest when he needed eternal tranquility instead. With a single claw, he pointed to his heart and looked at the gun in Nikolas's hand. "Please."

34

Dragging the limp body of a 275 pound werewolf and then lifting it into a truck for transport proved to be quite difficult. Not only was it heavy and frightening to look at, but actually having to touch its rough fur was much worse than they had expected it to be. As Deidra looked on from a safe distance on that small cliff, Edward and her brother assisted Nikolas in carrying the beast. They placed it into the back of the enclosed green and white government truck. The agents then secured the back door in complete silence.

When Edward took his place again next to her in the dark blue SUV, he could only look into her eyes just long enough to convey a mixture of sadness and terror. The ride to the church was without conversation. Only a few instructions had been given—street names and suggestions on how parking in the shadows would be best. Along the way, Edward gazed into the streets of the small city that seemed stuck in a more innocent time. It was only when they had pulled up to the church that he appeared ready to deal with their reality again.

The sergeant parked them as far toward the back as possible and underneath a scattering of pecan trees. There were only a few older houses nearby that might contain potential witnesses. A small dog barked at their strange vehicles, doing its best to alert someone to their unwelcomed presence.

Edward turned to Deidra after seeing that the rest of their group was already preparing to enter the church. "He had a smell. It was … different," he told her.

The sympathy she felt for him showed in her eyes. "Yeah. He is different. Are you all right?"

"Yes," he replied unconvincingly. "Just … you know."

"I know," she responded before they exited the SUV and quickly followed their group into the church that had been left unlocked and ready for them, at Martin's personal request.

"Let's lay him out in front of the altar," Nikolas said. He was out of breath and concentrating on his every step as he cradled the listless head of the man whom he knew, someplace inside, was still Fernando.

"And Vincent?" Edward asked from behind the group of men struggling with the werewolf.

"Sit him on a bench," Nikolas called back.

Deidra guided Vincent to the front row of the church and sat next to him. Edward took a seat on the other side to help prop Vincent up.

"It's a pew," Martin corrected. He stepped backward from Fernando's limp body and rubbed his forearms to help relieve them of their soreness.

"Right. Sorry, Father." Nikolas searched the inside of the large church, assessing its layout. "You ready?"

"Don't have much of a choice, brother," Martin replied, clutching the book of Roman Ritual in his hand.

Nikolas made himself stand taller and took in a breath for strength. "I need you two to stand guard outside. Look natural. Like you're on duty," he said to the Border Patrol agents.

"Yes, sir," they both responded.

"Do not leave the area without my permission. There will be a debriefing before you are released," he warned.

"Yes, sir."

"I would like you two," Nikolas pointed at the men on loan to them from the Air Force, "to stand guard from the inside of the church. I want one of you at the front entrance, and one at the side where we came in."

"Yes, sir."

He didn't trust them or their superiors at the moment, but his options were limited. Surely, they had to be afraid for their lives, having seen a werewolf and a man his group claimed to be possessed, all in the same evening. Now, standing guard inside an old Catholic church, they had to be wondering, what on earth, or beyond, could happen next. All of that considered, Nikolas was confident enough that they would probably continue taking orders from him. At least for the time being.

As the agents in the olive-colored uniforms exited the building and the M-4 clad soldiers took to their posts, Nikolas nodded and stood aside and out of Martin's way. Martin steadied his hands to open the book of Roman Ritual while glancing at the suffering, hairy creature sprawled out before him.

He looked back to see Edward and Deidra seated on either side of Vincent. "Do I begin?" he asked them.

Deidra perked up, causing Vincent to slump over to the side a bit and onto Edward's shoulder. "Yes, I guess so," she replied shakily.

Something over Deidra's shoulder, at the back of the church, caught Martin's attention. A light, bright and glowing, from inside the confessional booth, caused his jaw to drop. "Look!"

The sergeant who had been guarding the front of the church, near the confessional, corrected his footing and walked toward the glowing light before stopping at a distance, to correct the grip on his weapon.

"Get back!" Nikolas yelled at the soldier.

Martin dropped to his knees beside Fernando, his lips quivering mercilessly. He could not take his eyes off of the bluish-white light that was now accompanied by a pulsating hum. The sound caused a low vibration to occur throughout the entire church, lightly shaking everything around them. Deidra rose to her feet and spun around, covering her mouth with her hand.

"Watch the door!" Nikolas yelled to the sergeant. He then turned to Deidra. "What's going on?"

"I don't know!" she managed to yell back.

Vincent then reached out for her leg. "Send Edward ... to the light," he groaned with great effort. His sunken eyes turned toward her. Deidra jumped back, horrified with the look on his face and the grittiness in his voice.

Martin looked to Edward for his reaction. Vincent struggled through the effects of the drug to lift his heavy head and met Edward's eyes. "They want you."

Edward felt numb.

"No harm will come to you. No harm ..." Vincent collapsed and Deidra quickly jumped to assist him before he slid from his seat and onto the ground.

Edward immediately looked at Martin for some guidance which he already suspected would not be there. Nikolas approached Edward from the side and waited anxiously to see what he wanted to do. Even with the immeasurable amount of fear in his eyes, Martin was able to produce a simple smile as a gesture of comfort for Edward's benefit. Edward could tell that Martin had something to say, but Nikolas got to him first.

"You need to go over there. We don't have a lot of time," Nikolas urged Edward.

"He doesn't have to do anything!" Deidra insisted. "Go put a bunch of bullets through that booth, Nik!"

"No!" Martin insisted. "You heard Vincent! Whatever it is ... it's not going to hurt him!"

The werewolf groaned in pain behind Martin.

"We're running out of time and sedatives!" Nikolas reminded them. "If we came here to help Fernando and Vincent, then that's what we're going to do! But right now, there's a freakish light coming from the back of this church. I think we need to address that issue first!"

The humming sound was beginning to make Edward feel light-headed. "I agree," Edward said to them while avoiding any eye contact. Reluctantly, he knew what he had to do. "I'll go see what it is."

His words were met with silence, followed by questioning glances. The only sounds, other than the persistent, low-frequency hum enveloping them, were the heavy, uneven breaths coming from Fernando. It was all that Edward could hear—painful gasps for air that accompanied the werewolf's suffering.

There was no objection to his decision. It made perfect sense to all of them. Whatever it was that was asking for Edward from within the light was obviously more powerful than they were. It had been specific and to the point. It—or they—wanted Edward.

Edward turned to Deidra. He could tell by the look on her face that she was sure something frightening was waiting for him within the dark, wooden booth. He held his hand out to her and, when she accepted it, pulled her in close to him.

She trembled in his arms. "Are you sure you want to—"

"I love you," he responded confidently. He kissed her gently on the lips.

When he pulled away, she reached out for him, afraid that whatever was back there might take him away from her, but Edward pulled her hand from his sleeve and smiled. Out of the corner of her eye, Deidra could see Nikolas sinking into himself. He was certain that Edward had won.

Edward turned and stood to walk down the aisle. Deidra's eyes swelled at the sudden painful memories of her and her siblings' First Confessions and the warm hand of her mother on her shoulder before she would enter the much dreaded booth. She could still see the plastic beads of her favorite pink crucifix resting on her nightstand and wished that she could remember the prayers she had recited so many times before bed as a child.

"Martin," Edward said, glancing at the book in the priest's hand. "Will you work with Vincent? It might help."

"Yes, Edward." Martin smiled back.

As Edward took his first step toward the back of the church, Martin edged in closer to Deidra. She let loose a sob and a display of soft but uncontrollable tears that he knew immediately to belong to the memory of their mother's passing. Nikolas instinctively moved back to keep watch on Fernando while keeping his eye on Edward's slow but steady progress toward the booth.

Halfway down the aisle, Edward could feel something watching him. A dark, but calm force pulled at him from within his chest. A tingling coolness seeped into his brain, surprising him at first but then calming him. It felt like a nurturing force. One that wanted to guide him—to prevent him from running away from what he was destined to face. It urged him to pull at the ornate wooden door of the booth. It was safe.

I can feel the eyes watching me, he thought as he entered and sat on the hard seat within. The wooden door closed and seemed to melt him into the darkness within. The glowing light that had been emanating from the attached compartment faded away until there was only blackness.

The stillness around him heightened his senses. Suddenly, he was contained within the confines of the booth, but also outside of it, floating in the quantum existence surrounding everything.

A pair of eyes in the adjoining compartment peeked at him through the lattice screen separating them, causing Edward to jump back. Intrusive, large, black eyes penetrated his thoughts and invited him to face his greatest fears. They offered him something, without a single word being said. They gave him a choice ... know truth, or reject it.

"God, please," Edward whispered. He could not turn to face it at that moment because he knew what it was. A grey.

Real, and in its natural alien form. It was not transparent or in disguise. Confusing Edward further was the undeniable feeling that this one felt different to him, causing him to wonder if there were different types of greys that he had not encountered before. There was a seriousness about this one that he did not feel around the others. Due to society relations, Edward had been exposed to greys on a regular basis, but they had not been like this one. This one didn't project a hyperactive vibe at all. It was calm and neutral.

The being leaned forward on its seat, and Edward could see the paleness of the skin on its shoulder–gleaming in the light coming through from the cracks of the doorframe. In fear, Edward pushed himself against the back of the booth as hard as he could. The wood creaked. The black eyes stared at him, patiently waiting for the calmness to set in.

"I don't ... you aren't like the others I've met. You don't feel the same. I'm scared," Edward explained, embarrassed with himself. "Sorry."

A set of pale fingers lightly pressed against the lattice.

Edward did his best to fight off the instinct to recoil. "Okay," he panicked and closed his eyes. His body shook as he raised his arm. He pressed the fingers of his right hand onto the tips of the pale fingers on the other side. Cold. Like a spark of fire ... electric energy shot through his veins and into his brain. A vision, like a movie ...

Her dress is the kind that twirls upward like a flower when it spins ... she's an angel. No ... she's a woman. She's beautiful. Her hair is dark, long ... shiny. Her smile is so soft.

Hotel. It's a nice room. There are trays out, like a meal was served. She is excited, but ... he is late. The food is now cold. Still, the beautiful woman is smiling and anxious. She's waiting. She's been waiting all day to tell him. It's news! He'll be there any minute ...

He arrives. She's talking. He doesn't seem happy though. He sits ... she's still smiling. She asks him if he's happy, and he pretends that he is. He looks down at her belly. It is growing. He can tell now. Life! She is so happy. She tells him it's life. My God ... the man ... it's Montemayor!

No ... not his wife. It's not his wife. It's someone else's wife. She's running water for a bath. He's upset ... she's getting in ... he's upset. The anger is growing. Bubbles. Now he's pushing her into ... the bubbles. No! The baby! No!

She's running in the park. He's chasing her ... laughing. He's remembering their love. He loved her. No! Not the baby!

Her face ... the eyes are open under the water, but she's not moving. He's closing them with his fingers so she won't look at him any longer. She's gone. The baby's gone ... oh, my God. She hardly fought him. Sadness. It's gone. Everything.

The pale fingers pulled away quickly, leaving Edward to wake from a trance that had caused tears to fall from his eyes and his mouth to gape open. His stomach was nauseated. He was dizzy. "He ... is being punished?"

Yes, it told him without a voice.

"Cursed?" Edward shivered. He was cold and more frightened than he had ever been in his life. "Deidra said it might be a curse. An ancient one."

It nodded once to mimic a human "yes."

"Anubis? To teach a lesson? To remind us of ... consequences," Edward continued.

The visitor waited patiently for him to make the connection on his own.

"But what happened with Vincent? Um ... the other guy we brought with us ..." Edward asked with shyness.

That was not us, the being answered again, voiceless. It then placed an instantaneous vision into Edward's mind in order to explain further. This time, the vision was not felt in the same way as the one he had with Montemayor. Vincent's story was dry and quick, over within seconds, like a VHS tape on fast forward.

After experiencing the dreamlike flash, Edward sat up straighter and turned toward the alien face next to him, concealed for the most part in the shadows of the booth. "But with Montemayor ... why? So many people kill and hurt others. Why curse only one?"

He froze. Something entered his mind, uninvited. A vision of greatness. Leadership. Strength. Something his planet needed. Something beginning once but now lost. "The baby," Edward whispered, holding back tears of realization. He closed his eyes in shame and moments later, upon opening them, he discovered that the being in the compartment next to him was gone.

It is with sadness that we must still bring monsters to life to instill fear in the corrupt ... and the innocent, a voice said into his mind. *The Great Seeker must guide and protect the afterlife. The afterlife is sacred.*

35

"I was tricked. They lied to me," Vincent explained unconvincingly to his audience crowded into the Tahoe.

Deidra smirked. She was unwilling to admit the happiness she felt in seeing the return of Vincent's overly animated personality, but hung on his every agitating word with renewed excitement. "You are insane. I hope you learned your lesson."

"Yeah. Don't let them inject me with the soul of an alien. Got it. It kinda sounded like a good idea at the time though. You gotta admit." Vincent looked around nervously from the back seat that he shared with Deidra and Edward. He kept peeking back to gaze at a hairy, monstrous creature he could hear struggling to breathe. "What did they do to *him*?"

Fernando had been gagged with a white t-shirt, handcuffed, and injected with another dose of morphine. When Edward had made his shaky exit from the confessional booth, the first thing he told them was that he wanted Fernando secured and placed into the back of the Tahoe. He then told Nikolas to debrief and dismiss their government help. He didn't want them involved in the next part of their mission. Nikolas then volunteered to drive them to wherever Edward had in mind.

"Don't worry about him," Edward advised. He smiled and turned to shake Vincent's hand. "I'm Edward, by the way."

"Is he a freakin' werewolf?" Vincent asked. He shook Edward's hand weakly, still feeling groggy.

"Yes."

"Cool! Nice way to meet you," Vincent snickered. "Is he yours?"

Martin turned from his place in the front passenger seat to study Vincent's face. "You are very fortunate, my friend." He then turned to Edward. "He snapped right out of it when you emerged from the booth."

"Instantly shot up in his seat," Deidra added. "Like the drug in his system meant nothing. Just ... back to normal! It was incredible!"

"But while you were in the booth, he did mumble on about a few things," Nikolas reminded them.

"Like what?" Edward asked.

"Oh, like how we'd better watch out, trust no one, blah blah blah," Deidra responded. "So, naturally, since Vincent got better, we expected the same thing to happen with Montemayor."

"Yeah," Martin answered with sadness. "So why didn't Fernando change back?"

Edward sighed and then glanced back at Fernando, squashed into the back section of the Tahoe with duffle bags and other odd pieces of luggage crowded around his disheveled body. "Because what was done to Vincent was an experiment. And possibly ... a sick form of revenge."

"Hey!" Vincent complained.

Edward paused before answering, trying to recall the images that flashed through his head in the confessional booth. "No offense, Vinny. But what they did to you wasn't the same as … what was done to Montemayor. Well … kind of. From what I understood, with you, it started out as a test. The intention was to take you, to race for them, but then sometime after the injection you crashed your car in some stupid street race and damaged your body. The alien personality, or soul, was already in you. So, when you hit your head in the crash, something went wrong. When things got bad, instead of helping you and taking the thing out, they just let it take its course. To punish me, I think. I'm sure our investors are pissed off at me and wanted to show us that they could take our racers from us if we didn't liven things up again … or that they could damage racers if they wanted to. I think what they did to you was to prove a point. To teach *me* a lesson. What was done to Montemayor was to teach humanity a lesson."

"So it wasn't my fault, right?" Vincent asked with uneasiness. "Thank God you guys got a priest to help me. I owe you guys. Didn't know you cared about me like that."

Edward wore a look of confusion. He avoided Martin's eyes as he looked past Vincent to scan Deidra's face for an answer. There was no way Martin's prayers would have worked to rid Vincent of the non-demonic possession. *But, technically, it was still a case of possession*, Edward remembered. And, at this point, he was way past realizing that almost anything was infinitely possible.

Deidra felt his stare on her and smiled. "It's true, Eddie. While you were in that booth, Martin prayed over Vincent the entire time. He finished seconds before you stepped out."

Martin grinned modestly. "They were pretty simple prayers. Nothing too intense."

"So, Martin brought Vincent back?" Edward asked. He was curious about Deidra's take on it.

"I think so," Deidra confirmed. "Did your big-eyed friend mention anything about how to fix Vincent while you were in there?"

"No," he recalled. "I just got a quick explanation about what had been done to him and how the group that did it didn't want him anymore after he crashed that night. I was shown everything all at once, though. Like a flash in my head."

"Then it probably *was* a group of pissed-off investors that messed with Vinny," she suggested. "And I'm still not convinced that they aren't up to something more. Something bigger."

"Or it was one of the rebel groups," Nikolas jumped in. "The ones that are against human-alien relations."

"So you *do* know some stuff." Deidra was impressed.

"What a bunch of freakin' jerks!" Vincent snapped angrily and slammed his fist into the console between Nikolas and Martin. "So they lied about the millions of dollars then, too?! They said I was going to be famous across the whole entire universe!"

Deidra burst out laughing.

Nikolas waited a few seconds for the laughter to die down before speaking. "So explain to me again what it is that we are going to do with Montemayor." He felt uncomfortable asking. They were all well aware that Fernando was still part human. Although drugged, he somehow seemed to understand that he was being transported someplace when they put him into the back of the SUV. He knew that the plans had changed.

"I gave him my word that I would help him," Martin explained with pain in his voice. "I must keep my word."

Edward leaned forward to answer them. "It's not what you think, Martin. He messed up. Bad. And I'm pretty sure he knows why this was done to him. I was ... shown what really happened."

"Do you trust what you were told or what you saw in that booth?" Nikolas asked.

"Yes," Edward answered. "It didn't feel deceptive at all."

Martin lowered his voice. "Are we going to set him free?"

"No," Edward said. "I ... I can't do that to people. I don't want anyone else hurt. I think ... I have a feeling that enough people saw him ... the werewolf ... to retell the tale. You know what I mean? That was the purpose. That's what they wanted from this. That's a part of what myths are. Lessons passed on."

Vincent shivered in his seat. "Damn. I'm sure glad they didn't werewolf *me*."

36

"Are you sure he's not ever changing back?" Deidra asked Edward for the second time since leaving the church.

"Yes. I can't explain how I know, but I do. It's permanent."

"They do creepy things like that to your head, Eddie," she explained with her finger pointed into the night sky and an uncomfortable grin on her face. "You know something, but you don't know how you know it." She shuddered.

Nikolas closed a pair of handcuffs to connect a few links together on a thick, metal chain that was wrapped around Fernando's waist and neck. They had taken the chain from an office inside the church. Martin guessed that it had probably been used in the past to secure the old doors on the front of the building, but Deidra had a different idea. She was almost certain that, with all the legends of monsters and mysterious creatures that had been floating around for centuries, the Church did not ignore them.

"If we had looked around a little harder, we probably would have found a crossbow in there," she told Martin. "Let's go back after this and check!"

"Deidra, please," Martin was filled with uneasiness. The entire situation sent guilt through his mind as he replayed the promises he had made to Fernando in his head. He could not face Fernando any longer. He tried as hard as he could to think of him strictly as a werewolf and not as a man, but it was difficult for him. "Is Nik finished yet?"

"Yes. Don't worry," Deidra tried softly. "It's either this … or he runs loose killing people."

Martin sighed. "Okay, but I don't understand why it has to be like … *this*. I just want to go."

Nikolas walked over to where they were standing, just feet away from where he had just finished securing Fernando. "You want to say a prayer for him first, Father?" he asked Martin respectfully.

Martin looked at Nikolas with horror in his eyes. "How can I … stand in front of him and … he's chained to the U.S. border fence!" He hissed in disapproval.

"You can give him his last rites, Martin. I think it might make both of you feel better," Nikolas added while shifting his eyes back to Fernando. "He hasn't bothered to fight what we're doing. He knows he's done. I think he wants it to end."

Martin looked down at his rough hands and then over to his sister. "I hope you guys are doing the right thing."

Martin then walked over to the werewolf and stood before it. It was chained to the black metal fence, fixed into a standing position. The werewolf's size was improbable and caused Martin to appear shrunken down in comparison. He made the sign of the cross and prayed for the beast, and for the man within. Martin held strong and fought through any doubt. He could see that the strength of the beast was, in fact, returning. If let loose, it would certainly hunt down and kill innocent people. He had to come to terms with that realization as he blessed the werewolf and prayed for his soul.

Edward stepped in close to Nikolas, waving Deidra and Vincent back to the Tahoe. "You've hunted around here before, right? Deidra mentioned something about it earlier," he asked Nikolas quietly.

"Yes."

"I'm sure you know some guys that would do anything for an exotic like this one."

Nikolas's eyes widened. His heart felt like it had skipped a beat as he contemplated Edward's suggestion. "You want me to call ... a hunter?"

"Someone local. Yes." Edward kept a stern expression on his face. He did his best to distance himself emotionally from the callousness of his idea. An idea that only he knew made perfect sense. "I can't have you do it. You knew him. And ... hunters have bragging rights. That might help keep the legend alive ... like they wanted. It's that, or let him loose. The story is supposed to be told."

"But this can't get out!" Nikolas stressed.

"It's supposed to get out the way other things do that we don't understand. By rumor. Some will believe and some won't. That's just the way it's supposed to be." Edward read the look of caution in Nikolas's face. "In the past, things like this would live on through the stories of victims. I don't want any more victims. We have technology now. There are other ways."

Nikolas leaned in closer to Edward's ear. "No matter who I call or how much I trust them to be careful about this, they will make a trophy out of him. And they'll probably be tempted to take a few photos with him as well. Photos that I can't promise won't be leaked on the Internet."

Edward looked deep into Nikolas's eyes. "Besides what he did out here to that federal agent, he killed a pregnant woman. He killed her while he was *Congressman* Montemayor. And when he killed her, he murdered his own unborn child. So, I don't care what they do to him. Just pick someone who can handle it without getting themselves into any trouble."

Edward walked toward the Tahoe and placed a hand on Deidra's shoulder, suggesting that they quickly prepare to leave. She looked warmly into Edward's eyes.

Nikolas watched as Martin stepped away from the werewolf. Emotions churned deep inside of him as he thought about a hunter he knew—a man that had helped train and guide him in the art of leadership at the beginning of his career. A fellow ex-law enforcement officer that was now retired and had become an avid outdoorsman. When he had left the police department years ago, he took out his entire savings and moved to a ranch in Del Rio because it had been his longtime dream to do so. He invited Nikolas to hunt with him whenever he wanted because he was "the best damned officer he had ever worked with." While they hunted, the man told him strange tales about the chupacabras and UFOs he was sure he had witnessed in the darkness of the desert. The man felt blessed because Del Rio had opened his mind to the unknown. He swore to Nikolas that he would catch one of those chupacabras one day because he knew that there was more going on in the world than most people could wrap their heads around. All he wanted to do was prove it someday. That was the way he wanted to be remembered, the man had told him. He wanted to be a part of the truth. But, Nikolas knew that his friend had recently been diagnosed with a terminal illness. Nikolas respected the man more than he could put into words and he was one of the few that knew about the position he had accepted with the government.

His friend would give anything to be a part of the secrets the world kept from him, but now his time was running out.

Nikolas brought his cell phone to his ear. "Hey there, Russell ... yeah, I know. It's been a while. Uh huh ... oh, my dad's fine. Same old stubborn guy he's always been. You've been feeling good? Things are ... the therapy is going okay? Uh huh ... that's great, man. I'm really glad to hear that. Listen, what I'm about to say is going to sound strange, but you're going to have to trust me. Get your shotgun and grab a good set of bolt cutters. I've got something here that I know will interest you."

Warning

Dear Reader,

The Secret Order for the Universal Study of the Afterlife Society does not exist. An increase in Internet searches for the organization and its members has been documented by various agencies. Let it be known that attempts to contact, seek out, or expose any member of the said non-existent organization, is strongly discouraged. Due to our state of non-existence, let it be known that we do not have any current or past relations with non-human beings. It is also careless and slanderous to believe that the said non-existent organization has an unhealthy obsession with vanilla cupcakes. No members exist. There is no Secret Afterlife Society. Do not seek us out. We do not control or manipulate the system. Mind your own business.

Thank you.

(name withheld)

p.s.

www.ingramcontent.com/pod-product-compliance
Lightning Source LLC
Chambersburg PA
CBHW021957170626
46808CB00001B/185